"But you're bringing her up like a boy!"

The words were out before Andrina realized how critical they must sound, but Ward Prentice laughed. "What would you have me do?" he asked with a dangerous glint in his eyes.

"Salty needs a home background," she said hesitantly. "A mother's influence."

He drew nearer, and her heart began to beat rapidly. "You talk like a self-righteous schoolma'am," he said. "Is that what you are? Or are you by any chance applying for the position of my wife?"

His vividly blue eyes were openly amused now, and Andrina declared angrily, "I would never do that! It would be the last thing on my mind."

"You're quite sure?" he asked mockingly as he clasped her arms, imprisoning her. Then he bent down and covered her mouth with his.

JEAN S. MacLEOD
is also the author of these
Harlequin Romances

Many of these titles are available at your local bookseller.

For a free catalogue listing all available Harlequin Romances
and Harlequin Presents, send your name and address to:

HARLEQUIN READER SERVICE,
M.P.O. Box 707, Niagara Falls, NY 14302
Canadian address: Stratford, Ontario N5A 6W2

Black Sand, White Sand

by

JEAN S. MacLEOD

Harlequin Books

TORONTO • LONDON • LOS ANGELES • AMSTERDAM
SYDNEY • HAMBURG • PARIS • STOCKHOLM • ATHENS • TOKYO

Original hardcover edition published in 1980
by Mills & Boon Limited

ISBN 0-373-02414-2

Harlequin edition published July 1981

CHAPTER ONE

IT was a long way to come to be stranded on an island jetty waiting for a disabled launch to take her to her destination.

Andrina Collington looked out across the blue water of the Caribbean Sea with the first hint of uncertainty in her eyes, thinking about the journey she had made in response to her aunt's letter. She had received the brief summons when she had needed something to hold on to, when she had been faced with two conflicting decisions, neither of which had really appealed to her, and the journey to the Caribbean had seemed a happy alternative.

'I need help,' her aunt had written. 'Since your uncle's death I've been quite alone here, trying to manage the hotel as best I can, but now I realise how difficult it is. I'm no longer young. Don't think that I've lost my enthusiasm for life—not so! I still love this island with all it has to offer and I wouldn't wish to live anywhere else, but something has cropped up—an inconvenience, I would call it— and I feel in need of support. Moral support, I suppose I mean. What I'm suggesting is that you should come out here and see me. Make it a holiday, if you like. I won't hold you to any promise made on the spur of the moment, but you are my only living relative, and that sort of thing begins to matter as one grows older.'

Aunt Belle, who had been Isabel Collington before her marriage to an American, had gone off to the United States with him when his tour of duty in Scotland had ended. Andrina and her father had heard from them from time to time, from California, and Dallas, and San Francisco and, finally, from the Caribbean where they had 'bought half an island' and settled down to the unlikely business of running a hotel. They had described their new

home as 'an earthly paradise' situated on one of the lesser
Grenadines, and Andrina had gazed down on the magic
chain of islands running in a diminishing line south and
west of Barbados with a quickening heartbeat and a deepening response to the beauty which lay beneath her.

The island plane had left Barbados less than an hour ago,
flying over a sea so vividly blue that the sky itself seemed
to have tumbled into it, and all the islands from Grenada
to St Lucia lay like green gems on its polished surface, making her wonder what could possibly have gone wrong in her
aunt's 'earthly paradise'. It had seemed quite perfect as a
gentle trade wind had fanned her cheeks as they had landed
on Grenada, and she had held her breath at the beauty
of it all as the hired car had hurtled along the palm-fringed
shore road to deposit her on the jetty where she had been
told to wait.

The launch she had expected was there all right, but
it seemed to be deserted. Going towards it, she was suddenly aware of a lethargy which she supposed she should
have expected. It was mid-afternoon and the signs of
activity were few and far between. The launch which lay
at the end of the jetty had been loaded with provisions,
crates of wine and a well-known brand of Scotch whisky,
and dry goods, together with nets of fresh vegetables from
the main island which were probably earmarked for her
aunt's hotel. Castaways, she understood, was the only
hotel on the island, and the thought momentarily crossed
her mind that they could have grown the papaya and yams
and bananas for themselves, but Aunt Belle had never been
a practical sort of person and they had never really known
her husband. Albert Speitz had been a large, hearty man
in his middle thirties when they had met, a man more concerned with ships than running a hotel for the very rich,
as Andrina expected Castaways would be, sited as it was
on her aunt's paradise island on one of the lesser Grenadines.

Shading her eyes with her hand, she gazed seawards to
where several islands were strung out along the horizon,

wondering which was Flambeau. The nearest one looked
too large, the most distant lost in the haze of a dazzling sun,
yet one of them was to be her home for at least a month,
the place where she hoped to come to terms with the future
and forget the past.

'You waitin' for Mr Fabian, ma'am?'

She turned back to the launch to encounter a pair of
black, shining eyes set in a bright face which crinkled instantly into an endearing smile. The voice had held all the
leisurely charm of the Islands and it was evident that the
speaker had been sound asleep somewhere when he had
not even heard the arrival of her taxi.

'Yes, I am,' she acknowledged, returning the smile. 'Do
you know where he is?'

The native youth removed his straw trilby to consider
her question.

'I know where he may have gone,' he said carefully, 'but
he done set out to look for a spare part a' right. He been
away a long time now,' he concluded, looking at the sun.

'How long?'

The boy shrugged his shoulders: time had no real meaning for him.

'One—maybe two hours.'

'Two *hours*!' Andrina glanced at her watch, looking
about her at the almost empty landscape. 'Has he gone to
St George's?'

Again the uncertain shrug while her new acquaintance
searched the horizon.

'Not so far, maybe. He come back soon.'

'How soon?'

'Before sun goes.'

Andrina continued to look about her with a certain amount
of impatience. The launch was the only craft lying at the
jetty, but out on the water, her paintwork shimmering in
the bright sunshine, a beautiful schooner lay at anchor, her
graceful bow and tall, raking masts dominating the scatter
of smaller vessels lying drowsily around her. None of them
seemed to be occupied, but by the signs of activity along

the schooner's deck it appeared that she was ready to sail.

'I must get to Flambeau,' Andrina told her dark-eyed acquaintance. 'I expected Mr Fabian to pick me up at three o'clock, but if he doesn't return I suppose I could be stranded here for the night.'

It was question and statement combined and he did not contradict her.

'Mr Fabian, he come back soon,' he repeated. 'He not start engine without part.'

'How far is it to Flambeau?' she asked, still looking at the schooner.

'Not far. When engine work properly it take one hour.'

Looking down at the shabby craft which was to carry her to her aunt's island paradise, Andrina had her doubts. The launch had seen better days, but now it was evidently used for carrying stores, with any passenger who wished to travel to Flambeau a very minor consideration indeed. There was a small wheelhouse aft, with most of the cargo space for'ard and a narrow plank seat circling the well which was already piled high with boxes and crates flung haphazardly on top of each other so that she would be lucky even to find standing-room on the crossing. The wheelhouse would hold no more than two and it would be the absent Mr Fabian who would occupy it in his rôle of skipper.

She asked the deck-hand his name.

'Josh,' he grinned obligingly. 'I Mr Fabian's right-hand man.'

'Do you also work for my aunt, Mrs Speitz?' Andrina enquired.

'We all work for Mrs Speitz,' Josh beamed. 'She ver' fine employer.'

'And Mr Fabian?'

'He Mrs Speitz's manager.'

'Oh?'

Her aunt had only mentioned Gerald Fabian in passing. 'He will pick you up and bring you across to the island,' she had written at the end of a page of detailed instructions on how to get to Flambeau. 'You'll like him.'

Age and pedigree had been forgotten, so there was no way of knowing what Mr Fabian would be like. If she had thought about him at all, Andrina had imagined something between an elderly beachcomber and an ex-mariner content to dream away the rest of his days on a sub-tropical island at her aunt's expense, but of course, she could be quite wrong. Her estimate of him could be completely unfair.

She looked back along the jetty with a slight frown marring her brow, a strand of her long auburn hair blown across her cheek by the wind that was no longer cool. In the full glare of the sun it was very hot and the small inter-island plane had been warm and stuffy at the end of her pleasant jet-propelled journey from London. She was suddenly conscious of the little beads of perspiration on her upper lip and the moisture of her palms as a vague feeling of anti-climax took possession of her and a momentary fear stirred in her heart.

'Mr Fabian wouldn't just have abandoned everything, would he?' she asked. 'Gone away, I mean, for several days.'

'Oh, no, ma'am,' Josh assured her instantly. 'He live on Flambeau. He been there a long time.'

He seemed confused and surprised that she should doubt Mr Fabian's loyalty to the island.

'Do you think I could sit in the wheelhouse out of the sun?' Andrina suggested.

Josh looked doubtful.

'De spirits in there—de whisky,' he enlarged for her benefit. 'It no good long time in sun. Mr Fabian, he move it when he come.' He indicated the narrow gangplank. 'Maybe you could sit behind wheelhouse,' he suggested. 'It not too warm there.'

Andrina looked down at her few belongings which the native taxi-driver had deposited on the jetty beside the few packages still to be loaded on to the island ferry.

'I wonder if there's going to be room for them,' she said doubtfully.

'Plenty room,' Josh assured her. 'Soon everything will

be shipshape. Mr Fabian want you to be happy,' he grinned obligingly.

'If "Mr Fabian" would only get here and show willing!' Andrina murmered, suddenly aware that the elegant schooner had up-anchored and was moving in towards the jetty where its occupants would no doubt land. In such a dignified craft they would be the usual wealthy holiday-makers cruising among the Islands, and somehow she did not want to meet a group of vivacious Americans or even her own countrymen in her present predicament.

'I'll come aboard,' she told Josh. 'Find me a cool spot on deck, if you can.'

Clambering over the inadequate gangplank, she was aware of being watched. The schooner was almost along-side and the tall man at the door of the chart-room was looking down on them from his superior height. For the briefest of moments their eyes met, his blue as the sun-kissed seas he sailed, hers darkly querulous, although he was a stranger and owed her nothing. Then he was look-ing away again, giving his undivided attention to the handling of his ship.

Andrina watched as he manoeuvred it alongside the jetty while a deckhand jumped ashore to secure the warps.

'It's beautiful!' she remarked to no one in particular, but Josh answered her, looking back along the deck.

'*Sea Hawk*,' he said. 'She big pirate ship once.'

Andrina wondered what he meant. There were no pirates left now, not even on the wide blue Caribbean where they had prospered so long ago.

'She run contraband up in de Virgins,' Josh explained. 'In among the cays. She good, fast ship to get away!'

Glancing once more at the man in the charthouse, Andrina could almost imagine him running the gauntlet of pursuit with a mocking gleam in his eyes, his curling lip showing his brief contempt for authority. His face was in profile now and she saw him as the sea pirate he might have been not so long ago, his deeply-tanned skin drawn sparsely across his high cheekbones, his jaw set

and angular, the eagle gaze scanning the horizon in a
wide, commanding sweep in search of prey. Somewhere
out there on the wide tropical sea was surely his natural
environment, with the wind filling the schooner's sails and
the waves rushing along its hull.

Josh helped her across the gangplank into the launch,
where she stood at the gunwale waiting for him to clear a
space for her to sit down. There wasn't really any space
until he had piled several crates on top of each other, and
this manoeuvre effectively cut off her view of the schooner
and the tall man in the charthouse. A deep, waiting hush
seemed to descend on the island behind them, a sense of
time suspended, an illusion that the passing hours were
irreverent intruders in the quiet of this tropical paradise.
Josh moved at such a leisurely pace that it was almost
sleepwalking, and she supposed she had interrupted a
pleasant afternoon sleep by her untimely appearance.

Beyond the jetty, valleys and mountain slopes clambering skywards on each other's shoulders were interspersed
by a wild tangle of tropical forest, green and lush and still
until the quiet was mercilessly shattered by the rough sound
of an engine and a mini-moke was driven recklessly off the
main road. It approached them in a series of jolts to be
finally brought to a halt inches from the end of their
gangplank.

'Mr Fabian!' Josh announced with an appreciative grin.

A man in faded jeans and a checked shirt open to the
waist jumped from the vehicle, signalling to the native
driver to wait. He was younger than Andrina had imagined,
with fair, curling hair which grew thickly into the nape
of his neck and green eyes which brightened perceptibly
when he saw her. Constant exposure to sun and wind had
burned his skin to a golden tan and he was still clean-
shaven. Somehow she had expected a beard. Not quite
'gone native', she decided as she noticed the shabby rope
sandals on his feet and the patch on his jeans.

'I did my best,' he announced with an enchanting smile
as he took the gangplank in his stride to shake her by the

hand. 'I heard in town that you'd hired a taxi, but I was held up at the garage.' He made a wry face. 'The launch is getting too old to pick up spare parts whenever they're needed,' he added, signalling to the driver that he could go.

'Don't you pay him?' Andrina asked, not quite knowing what to make of this inconsequential newcomer.

'It goes on the bill,' he said, lightheartedly dismissing the debt. 'We hire the Moke from the garage when we need it. Everything's fair and above board.' The green eyes squinted up at her in the sunshine. 'Had a pleasant journey?'

'Very.' She hesitated. 'Mr Fabian, is there any way of letting my aunt know we've been held up?'

He looked surprised.

'Not really. She'll expect us when we get there.'

'I see. All the same, I would prefer it if she knew what had happened. How long will you be?'

He turned away to hide a smile.

'Time is of no consequence here,' he said.

'So I've gathered, but there's the point that my aunt might feel a certain amount of anxiety if we don't put in an appearance before dark.'

He rubbed his chin, on which a fine growth of stubble was taking over.

'Not to worry,' he said lightly. 'I'll work on the engine for the rest of the afternoon and then we can drift across to Flambeau in the moonlight!'

'Don't joke! I really do feel concerned about my aunt. Surely you have a radio or something?' she suggested.

'Alas,' he shrugged, 'that, too, needs some attention on the receiving end. Crises are something we don't consider till they actually happen.'

'This is something of a crisis,' she reminded him. 'Are you sure you can mend the engine during the afternoon?'

'I'll do my best.' His sideways glance was analytical, the green eyes taking in her trim linen suit and the long, slender legs he had first noticed as he had crossed the gangplank.

'Relax, Miss Collinton. At a pinch, we can sleep aboard.'

Aware of the derisive grin, Andrina knew that he was teasing her, and no doubt she had made too great a fuss about her delayed departure for the island, but she was tired after her long journey and it was natural enough for her to worry about her aunt.

'Perhaps you could get help,' she suggested.

He looked back along the deserted jetty.

'Not a chance,' he decided. 'Besides, I'm fairly competent—a first class engineer, in fact!'

The recommendation made her wonder what he was doing in a place like Flambeau.

'I hope so,' she said almost dryly.

Gerald Fabian reached out to touch her hand.

'Trust me,' he said, the green eyes mockingly bright. 'I never make a promise I'm not prepared to keep. There's food on board, by the way, and plenty to drink. Make yourself at home.'

He moved among the boxes, clearing a way for her to the wheelhouse which was so small and cramped that producing even a cup of tea would be an achievement worthy of note.

'I'm very thirsty,' she admitted. 'Could I have something to drink? Orange juice or—or tea.'

'There's a stove in the corner and a kettle somewhere,' he answered vaguely. 'There's also passionfruit juice and lime, or would you prefer something stronger?'

'I've never tasted passionfruit——'

He gave her an odd glance.

'I'd stick to lime or tea, in that case,' he said. 'I'll find some spirit for the stove. We don't drink tea, as a rule.'

'Mr Fabian,' said Andrina, 'I don't want to be a nuisance. I'll settle quite happily for lime.'

He found an unopened bottle at the back of a cupboard, holding it out to her.

'There should be a glass somewhere,' he decided.

'A mug will do.'

She had noticed several on the shelf behind him, dangling on a row of plastic hooks, and was half prepared for his raised eyebrows and the look of consternation in his eyes.

'That would never do,' he declared. 'We must treat our honoured guests with decorum.'

When he handed her the glass he had polished on a none-too-clean tea-towel she imagined that his expression had sharpened, the green eyes suddenly tinged with reserve.

'I'm hardly a guest,' Andrina reminded him. 'I intend to help my aunt with the hotel while I'm here, if she needs me.'

When he had poured the lime he turned to put the bottle back in the cupboard which was fitted with a wooden rack to prevent movement in a turbulent sea, and she found herself gazing at the back of his neck where the thick hair grew down to a natural peak, just failing to conceal the rough scar which slanted to his shoulder on one side. It was something so out of keeping with his otherwise perfect body that she felt curiously repelled by it, but in a second he had turned and she was looking into the fascinating green eyes again.

'Come on deck when you're ready,' he invited. 'It's stuffy in here.'

Andrina drank the cooling lime in long, satisfying gulps, aware of how thirsty she had been. It was three hours since she had left the airport in the dusty taxi which she had hired to bring her to the jetty on this northernmost part of the island and she had been too busy admiring the scenery on the way to recognise her thirst. Grenada was a temptress, stealing away your thoughts with her wild, volcanic mountains and green forests plunging down to bays of incredible beauty where white surf broke incessantly on golden sand and the sea was a turquoise dream. More than once she had asked the native driver of her car to stop so that she might gaze down towards a palm-fringed shore or up into a lush valley to a shady grove of nutmeg where the sunlight seemed to be trapped in a golden haze between the trees. It was something hitherto unknown to her and she hoped fervently that Flambeau would be the same. Smaller, of

course, for it was one of the lesser Grenadines, but she had
no doubt that it would be equally beautiful.

Rinsing out the glass at the small sink next to the stove,
she set it to drain on the rack provided for the purpose before she ventured on deck again. Gerald Fabian and Josh
had disappeared.

Where could they possibly have gone on a jetty that
boasted neither a hut nor a store of any description?
Civilization seemed to be concentrated on the southern part
of the island and in the interior where a high volcanic peak
dominated the landscape. It was almost three thousand feet
high, she guessed, looking up at it and seeing the first tiny
cloud she had noticed since her arrival resting on its forehead.

'Having trouble?'

A man's voice, half amused, half impatient, broke the
silence as she looked up to discover the skipper from *Sea
Hawk* standing on the jetty above her, and almost simul-
taneously Gerald Fabian stuck his head out of the well
where he had been contemplating the reluctant engine
hidden from view by the bulk of the cargo.

'What do you want?' he asked ungraciously, glaring at
the older man.

'I wondered what you needed that took you off into town
in such a hurry. Perhaps, if you'd asked, I could have
helped.'

Their eyes met with the glint of steel on steel. There was
no love lost between them, Andrina decided.

'I can manage quite well on my own.' Gerald Fabian
wiped his brow with the back of his hand, leaving an oily
streak which seemed to emphasise the impatience of his
frown. 'After all, I had no idea you'd be around, waiting to
come to my rescue.'

The skipper of *Sea Hawk* allowed himself the briefest of
smiles, standing his ground above them, waiting to be
introduced.

'Miss Collington,' Gerald announced reluctantly. 'She's
coming to stay at Castaways.'

'You're Mrs Speitz's niece,' the older man said, eyeing her speculatively as he saluted her with a brevity which seemed to characterise all his actions. 'My name is Prentice,' he added. 'Ward Prentice. I live on Flambeau and I'm your aunt's nearest neighbour.'

But not exactly her friend, Andrina thought, unable to dismiss the suggestion of enmity in the atmosphere as the two men continued to eye each other across the width of the deck. Whatever had been between them in the past, there was certainly distrust of each other's motives now.

Suddenly taken aback by this strange encounter, she found herself avoiding the blue, searching gaze of the man on the jetty, trying to dismiss something which refused to be thrust aside, and instantly his eyes met hers, strongly demanding.

'*Sea Hawk* will be sailing in half an hour,' he said. 'If you're worried about the delay I'll take you across to Flambeau. Would you like me to radio your aunt in the meantime?'

'There's no way,' Gerald Fabian said aggressively. 'Our receiver is on the blink.'

The other man did not seem unduly surprised.

'I'll be in touch,' he said, turning away.

'Didn't he just love that!' Gerald snapped, grasping a spanner until his knuckles showed white against his tanned skin. 'Everything on *Sea Hawk* runs like clockwork and he has to show his superiority. Ill get this damned thing going if it's the last thing I do,' he added, setting to work again. 'I can't give him the satisfaction of proving he was right.'

'About the launch?'

'About everything!' Gerald declared. 'He thinks we don't run Castaways as efficiently as we should and he believes we could make better use of the land, but the whole point about an island like Flambeau is its—restfulness, that nobody makes too great an effort to streamline the place into a carbon copy of the next island or the one after that. It has its own particular character. If you take that away you'll ruin everything.'

'Is that what Mr Prentice wants to do?' Andrina asked slowly. 'Change Flambeau completely?'

'Out of all recognition. He runs his part of the island with clockwork precision, growing bananas and cocoa and spices on every available inch of his plantation while he organises the fishing and markets the Caribs' produce to bring in the greatest profit. Some of it for himself, of course.'

'How near a neighbour is he?' asked Andrina, sitting on the deck above him to watch his progress with the recalcitrant engine.

'Near enough to be fully aware of everything we do,' Gerald told her. 'On an island barely eight miles wide by twelve long it's difficult to avoid one's neighbour even though you have very little in common, and Prentice would be a lot happier if we didn't exist. He lives like a hermit half the time and the other half he's off on *Sea Hawk* on business of his own. It's as if he had two identities.' The green eyes narrowed. 'Doctor Jekyll lives on Flambeau, while Mr Hyde goes to sea.'

She thought that he exaggerated, aware of his almost primitive dislike of the older man who had acquired a great deal more of this world's goods than he had, and Ward Prentice's striking looks would always single him out from lesser men, which seemed to rankle where her aunt's assistant was concerned.

Once again she wondered what had brought Gerald to Flambeau and what had made him stay there for so long. She did not wonder about Ward Prentice because she knew why he preferred to own half of her aunt's island paradise and why he was in his element when he roved the blue Caribbean Sea. It was his natural habitat; the place where he knew himself to be free and the master of his own destiny whatever he chose to do. This fascinating man was in full command of his own future, but the trouble was that he might sweep others along with him into deep water.

She shivered at the thought, conscious of the sudden cold little wind which blew against her cheek, chilling her as she stood there gazing back at the mountains. The Islands could be cruel as well as kind and she had no desire to see their darker face.

For over an hour Gerald wrestled with the engine, but even after the new part had been installed it failed to respond to the starter.

'Damn you—work!' he exclaimed after several abortive efforts. 'I can't find anything else wrong.' He stood up, wiping his brow.

'Have we enough fuel?' Josh enquired helpfully.

'Of course we have enough fuel! I'm not completely stupid,' Gerald shouted. 'If you wouldn't just stand there looking on we might get something done!'

Josh, who had been handing this and that on cue, looked mortified.

'I's doin' my best, Mr Fabian,' he protested. 'I cert'nly am, but this dam' engine he no want to start anyway. No, sir! He jus' determined to not go an' that makes yo' angry, but maybe we could ask Mr Prentice to send over his man fro' *Sea Hawk*. He ver' good engineer——'

'Shut up, and hold this,' Gerald interrupted. 'You talk a lot of rubbish at times, Josh.'

Andrina glanced at her watch. It was getting late and already the sun was well down towards the horizon. Her aunt would have been waiting for her since three o'clock, worrying now that there was no sign of the launch approaching the island.

'Do you think you're going to make it?' she enquired tentatively, when Gerald Fabian looked up to smile at her.

'Before dark, do you mean? No, I don't think so,' he said. 'I'll have to strip this whole thing down again. It's a nuisance, but it can't be helped. We'll cross in the moonlight!' The green eyes twinkled as he looked at her.

'But supposing you don't get it started?' she objected.

'I can offer you a berth of sorts in the wheelhouse.'

It was most unsatisfactory, although he seemed to be treating their predicament with a wry sort of humour which eventually infuriated her.

'I wish we could have some sort of decision,' she said. 'It's getting late.'

Subconsciously she glanced along the jetty to where the schooner was still moored and was not surprised to see Ward Prentice coming towards them.

'You've given it a fair trial,' he said to Gerald. 'I'll send Garson over to have a look at it and Miss Collington can come with me. You can bring Garson over in the launch when you come,' he added with the air of a man used to giving orders which were not likely to be disobeyed.

'If it's not going to take too long I'd rather wait,' Andrina said defensively. 'There's no reason why I should put you to any trouble, Mr Prentice.'

'If you were doing that I wouldn't have suggested it.' The level blue gaze swept over her critically. 'You look tired and in need of a wash after your journey. All I'm offering you is a speedier trip to Flambeau and a sure landfall.'

The studied indifference of his tone sent a warm colour into her cheeks.

'If I didn't think my aunt might be anxious about me I would prefer to wait,' she said abruptly.

'You could wait all night and still be in the same invidious position in the morning,' he pointed out. 'Make up your mind. I'll be sailing in ten minutes if you want to join me.'

'See what I mean?' Gerald remarked as the skipper of *Sea Hawk* turned away. 'He'll do you a favour, but he'll make you aware of it.' He wiped his hands on an oily rag. 'You've got exactly ten minutes to make up your mind. No more, no less.'

Andrina hesitated.

'It feels like desertion,' she said. 'I wish I could have helped, but there's nothing I can really do.' Again she looked towards the graceful schooner lying behind them. 'I really ought to go, especially when we can't get a radio message to my aunt.'

He straightened his shoulders to look at her, an odd expression in his eyes.

'I suppose you should,' he said. 'I'll work at this till I get it right, but it *could* be tomorrow before we get back.'

'I'll tell my aunt.' She still felt half guilty of desertion. 'Could Josh bring my luggage?'

He nodded, obviously disinclined to board the schooner unless by the owner's invitation.

'You'll be on Flambeau in under an hour,' he said. '*Au revoir* for the present!'

Dismissed, Andrina walked slowly along the jetty, passing the crew member who was apparently Garson on the way. The tall young Bajan saluted her respectfully.

'Mr Prentice be waiting for you, ma'am,' he said.

Andrina could see Ward Prentice standing at the head of the narrow gangway he had put down to accommodate her, obviously expecting her capitulation. If there'd been any other way, she thought, I would have taken it.

'Come aboard,' Ward Prentice invited conventionally when she reached the gangway. 'Garson will take care of your baggage.'

'I've asked Josh to bring it along.'

He nodded.

'As you wish. I've told Garson to stay with Fabian and come over with the launch in the morning.'

'You don't think they'll be able to find the fault before that?'

'I doubt it.' His lip curled. 'Fabian will probably go back to St George's.'

'I think he'll work on the engine for as long as he can,' Andrina defended Gerald Fabian, 'and he can't very well leave all these stores unattended.'

'Josh will take care of them. He's a dependable type.' He turned to give his orders to the other deck-hand as Josh came aboard with her luggage and Garson stood ready to cast them off. 'Put them in the saloon, Josh,' he directed. 'Is this all you have?' He looked round at Andrina, faintly surprised.

'I travel light,' she said, watching Josh going back down

the gangway. 'I understand you don't dress for dinner on Flambeau.'

He laughed, revealing strong white teeth between his straight, firm lips.

'Hardly! One or two misfits have been known to bring the usual sophisticated clobber to wear at the hotel, but on the whole they adapt very well.'

He started the engine and they began to slip away from the jetty, noisily in reverse at first and then on a steady, powerful beat which set *Sea Hawk*'s prow northwards in among the islands.

There were no passengers on the trip. *Sea Hawk* was going home.

Andrina leaned against the chart-room, watching the jetty recede behind her with the two figures of Josh and Garson silhouetted against the island green. Gerald Fabian had decided not to see them off. Somewhere among the piles of crates and boxes he was labouring to prove himself as efficient an engineer as the man whose help he had contemptuously refused.

Alone with *Sea Hawk*'s skipper, she was suddenly aware of their isolation. Here, in this wide blue sea, they moved in a world of their own where Ward Prentice's word was undoubtedly law. He made room for her to sit down beside him, but she preferred to stand on deck, allowing the gentle trade wind to cool her cheeks.

'How long will you stay on Flambeau?' he shouted against the beat of the engine.

'I came for a month's holiday.'

'But you could stay longer?' The blue eyes searched hers.

'If my aunt needed me.'

'You're her only relative?'

'Yes. She has no children of her own. I think she must be very lonely at times.'

'What did you do in England?' he demanded. 'Have you a job to go back to?'

'No.' She felt the colour rising in her cheeks, the past catching up with her. 'I was a secretary, but I left my employment three weeks ago.'

'Which means that you could stay on Flambeau for more than your stipulated month?'

'I suppose so.' Suddenly she looked straight into the magnetic blue eyes. 'Why are you asking so many questions, Mr Prentice?' she demanded. 'Are you trying to tell me something about my aunt?'

He shook his head.

'I wondered about your background,' he said. 'That was all.'

It was presumptuous enough in a total stranger, Andrina decided, unless he had something definite to offer about life on her aunt's 'island paradise'.

They were threading their way through a chain of islands lying like anchored ships on the turquoise water and she moved along the deck to see them to greater advantage. Ronde and Carriacou, Union and Cannouan and distant, shadowy Mustique, with Bequia no more than a grey wraith in the distance. They all had their own particular characteristic, she supposed, and between them were the lesser isles, linking them in a magic chain, one to the other.

'Which is Flambeau?' she asked when Ward Prentice came to stand beside her.

'Over there.' He pointed. 'You can just about see it on the horizon.'

She looked without being able to see anything but the gathering haze of evening, but even from this distance she was aware of mystery, with a wild magic associated with far-away places which had always been in her blood.

The deck-hand had taken his place in the wheelhouse and he turned to run up a sail, catching the light trade wind as the engine cut out with dramatic suddenness, leaving them in a silence which could almost be felt. Andrina looked up at the shrouds with a sense of excitement, the impression of being carried forward to some strange destination which she could not escape. *Sea Hawk* picked up the wind with a gentle sigh, gliding like a phantom ship across a radiant sea.

'Why Flambeau?' Andrina asked when Ward Prentice rejoined her at the rail.

'If you look closely when we're near enough you'll see,' he assured her. 'This is the right time to come, when the sun sets and you see the whole dramatic effect of colour and light across the water. You would have missed it if you'd come earlier, or stayed overnight on Grenada.'

He looked down at her for her reaction to his statement and she said abruptly:

'I would have gone back to St George's. I had no intention of spending an uncomfortable night on board the launch.'

If he had been asking a tentative question he had been supplied with an answer. She was not the usual 'island-hopper', prepared to share a cabin with anyone.

He shifted his position to adjust the sail and she asked her own question.

'Do you trade among the Islands, Mr Prentice?'

He laughed.

'In a sort of way. I make *Sea Hawk* work for her living when I can.'

'Cruising?'

'Occasionally.'

She looked up at the soaring masts, seeing the full sail filled with the gentle wind which bore them forward effortlessly, feeling the silence close about them and watching as the sun grew into a huge orange ball to falter on the horizon for a second and then drop dramatically out of sight. Fascinated, she saw a sudden flash of vivid green light before the flame of the aftermath shot up from the sea. They stood on the deck, shoulder to shoulder as the colour deepened, consumed by it as if it had been a fire, silent, almost unmoving in the dramatic stillness.

'Over there,' said Ward Prentice at last. 'Does that answer your question about Flambeau?'

Ahead of them a small, dark island lay in the path of the approaching light, dramatically high at its western end, with a rugged chain of mountain peaks dropping down to a long peninsula, the 'handle' of the torch where lush tropical growth swept towards hidden coves of white coral sand fringed by slanting palms. The sun had left the island in a misty haze, but the high ridge of the mountains was burning with brilliant colour, the flame which gave Flambeau its dramatic name.

'Is it always like this?' Andrina asked, speaking in a whisper as if to preserve the silence and beauty of what she saw.

He shook his head.

'Not always. You're privileged tonight, but this is how I first saw it and how I'll always remember it.'

'If you leave it, do you mean?'

'For the present,' he said, 'I've made it my home.'

She turned from her contemplation of the glowing torch.

'You sound—satisfied,' she suggested. 'Is there enough to keep you busy on the island?'

'Not always.' He was gazing towards the shore. 'I hope to expand in due course.'

They dropped into the lee of the island, losing some of the wind as they ran along the shore. She could see the mountains more clearly now, jagged peaks spearing the sky with the colour gone from them and their shadow falling darkly over the land.

'You don't consider it too remote?' she was prompted to ask.

'Remoteness is a frame of mind.' He stood with one foot on the gunwale, gazing towards the highest peak. 'I never see myself as one of the crowd, but that doesn't mean to say I'm not involved. This island has been allowed to run to seed in the past, but I'm part-owner of half of it, and I'm trying to do something about it.'

'If that's a reflection on my aunt's ownership I resent it,' Andrina returned quickly. 'She's been left a widow and I'm sure she's doing her best at Castaways.'

'I don't doubt her good intentions.' He continued to gaze at the mountains. 'Castaways is highly successful in living up to its name. It's what she's doing with the land she owns that angers me.'

'Which means that you'd like to have it for yourself?'

Her tone was dry and he looked down at her, the blue eyes as hard as steel.

'That is what you'll be told,' he said briefly. 'Among other things. I can't expect you to like me, Miss Collington, since you're going to live at Castaways, but I would remind you that any enmity there might be between your aunt's hotel and my own plantation is not of my choosing. Mrs Speitz has her advisers and I would caution you to beware of them.'

His words fell into a silence which Andrina found hard to break. Was he referring to Gerald Fabian when he warned her about her aunt's 'advisers'? But Gerald was no more than her aunt's employee, a beachcomber who could have no real influence with Belle Speitz since they were not even related. It was a puzzling situation to meet head-on at the beginning of her holiday, but surely not one which could deeply concern her.

'I'll only be here for a short while,' she told her silent companion. 'I can't see that it really concerns me too much.'

He leaned with his back against the gunwale, considering her with the glow of the aftermath all about them turning his face to a deep bronze. An evil face? No, she decided. Strong and completely ruthless might be the better summing up. He moved his position to gaze at the island again and it seemed that he had come very near in the stillness as she felt a sudden, strange attraction to this man who had come into her life so unexpectedly. It was as if time had been suspended and completely forgotten as Flambeau took shape ahead of them, the shadow of the mountains darkening its rugged coastline and seeming to stretch out towards them as they approached. Yet they were still in the fiery light of the departing sun, its roseate glow touching the schooner's sails as she set in towards the shore.

It was then that Andrina saw the narrow beach with tall coconut palms lying aslant it and a white crest of foam breaking against a distant reef. It was all that she had imagined her aunt's island paradise to be, only the pale coral sand seemed to be whiter, the palms greener and the shadow they cast deeper. No cloud marred the sky; nothing but perfection seemed to reign amid so much beauty, but where was Castaways?

They went in through a gap in the reef where she could see the coral on either side of them, stretching away beneath the crystal-clear water at the entrance to the bay.

'Can we see the hotel from here?' she asked, breaking the spell which had wrapped them round for the past few minutes.

'Not quite. It's further along the beach, but I had to come in at the gap in the reef. Even with a gentle wind blowing it's safer than going round at the Bluff.'

'Does that mean I've taken you out of your way?' she asked.

'Not too far. I live on the other side of the island—the Atlantic side—but I often use the cove in a strong wind. It's the better harbour.'

Andrina looked at him quickly. Could this be at least part of his reason for criticising her aunt so strongly? Did he want to enlarge and maybe modernise this lovely stretch of sheltered and unspoiled lagoon? Reason enough, she supposed, if he had been a dedicated businessman, but he had just denied such a suggestion, his keen gaze fastening on the distant ocean beyond the reef. He wanted the island to remain as it was, remote and aloof and his alone.

The aftermath of sunset had faded and a dim, silvery light was taking its place, turning the green world ahead of them to a shadowy place full of magic, and she recognised the same magic in the nearness of Ward Prentice. It tore her thoughts from the reality of the present, casting them back to the past. She had vowed that she would never again fall in love so easily. Never again would she trust anyone wholeheartedly, as she had trusted Don.

Looking up at the strange, withdrawn man by her side, she saw him as dangerous, a man with a secret or a past so dark that he wished to forget it for all time. Stern-visaged, he stared at the sea, at the island he said meant so much to him, and then suddenly he was taking in the sail and the schooner, lost to the wind, was hovering like some giant black bird over the gentle water of the lagoon. She heard the rattle of the chain as the anchor went down, thinking that this might be the last time she would sail to Flambeau in such a romantic way.

At one end of the beach there was a rickety landing-stage made of rough planks and cross-pieces which had been restored haphazardly from time to time. Two flat-bottomed dinghies were moored at the end of it and a red-and-yellow sail-boat was drawn up on the sand under the palms.

'There you are!' said Ward Prentice at her elbow. 'Castaways in all its glory!'

'But—the hotel?' Andrina protested. 'There's nothing to be seen.'

A belt of lush vegetation stretched right down to the sand, covering the hillside for as far as she could see.

'It's there all right,' her companion assured her, 'in among the trees.'

The long strip of white sand looked so beautiful that she wanted to run along its pristine length barefooted and as free as the wind, but the pale light in the sky had almost gone and she knew that would have to wait for another day.

'I'll row you ashore since there seems to be nobody about,' Prentice offered. 'They haven't seen us coming in.'

'They would be expecting the launch.'

'No doubt.' The deck-hand had lowered a dinghy and they went aft to climb down to it by a rope accommodation ladder which made Andrina think of pirates. 'If you'll let me go first I'll make sure you don't fall into the sea.'

For the first time his tone was friendly, half-teasing, half-serious as he helped her into the smaller boat which seemed to plunge madly as she settled herself in the stern.

'Not far to go,' he said, pulling on the oars. 'Do you like the sea?'

'I've never been out in a small boat before,' she had to confess. 'I'm a Londoner.'

He looked sympathetic.

'Not even in the Park?' he wondered.

'Oh, that!' she smiled. 'It was a very long time ago. My cousin tipped me into the water and I suppose I never got over my fright. Or perhaps it was just that my dignity was severely damaged. I was eight.'

'Impressions linger,' he said. 'Sometimes for a very long time.' She thought he was frowning. 'A child's love of the sea can often be reversed by an unfortunate experience. It can leave a lasting impression which no amount of reassurance will ever conquer. It's the same with fire,' he added harshly. 'They're both natural elements beyond our control.'

'Like air and wind,' she agreed. 'But I can imagine you sailing *Sea Hawk* in all sorts of weather and revelling in the challenge.'

'It's my way of life, or has been up till a year ago,' he said. 'I chartered round the Islands before that and then I bought *Sea Hawk*. Unfortunately, I inherited her reputation with her,' he remarked dryly. 'She ran contraband at one time and was impounded, but she's a wonderful old girl. She's never let me down in all the time I've had her.' He looked back across the darkening lagoon to where the schooner lay silhouetted against the reef. 'I still work the odd charter,' he said, 'but only occasionally.'

'You have other work to keep you busy on Flambeau, I suppose.'

'A great deal of work,' he agreed, straightening his shoulders, 'and that, too, is something of a challenge.'

'I know you're not in the hotel business because Castaways is the only hotel on the island, so what do you do?' she found herself asking.

'I try to manage an estate. It's a job I've—given myself to do, and I mean to make a success of it, although it may not be entirely my cup of tea.'

'Living ashore, do you mean?'

He nodded.

'I suppose I had to come to it sooner or later,' he allowed, 'but the transition period wasn't easy. I valued my freedom, you see, and I'd made up my mind that it was the only thing that counted.'

'You never fell in love?'

It was an outrageous question to ask which she regretted immediately.

'Falling in love has never been my strong point,' he informed her icily. 'I've never seen it work for very long. Have you?'

She gazed back into the ice-blue eyes which were surely mocking her.

'Quite often,' she said. 'My father and mother were deeply in love.'

' "Were"?' he queried.

'They died a short time ago. My mother first and then my father.'

'Is that why you've come out here?'

'Not exactly, but my aunt wrote and asked if I would like a holiday and at that time I needed one. It was very kind of her, especially as we hadn't met for years.'

'She has no family of her own, I understand. I wonder if it's wise for her to stay here.'

Andrina stiffened.

'I wouldn't dream of offering her that kind of advice,' she said.

They had reached the landing-stage and she held on to it as Ward Prentice shipped his oars and prepared to step ashore with her.

'I can manage all right if you tell me where the hotel is,' she assured him. 'It can't be far to walk.'

'It isn't, but you'll still need someone to carry your luggage.' The deck-hand had put her suitcase in the dinghy as they had left the schooner and she had rested her canvas holdall on her knees on the short trip across. 'Castaways is a series of thatched bungalows in there among the trees,' her escort explained. 'A sort of do-it-yourself idea, but there's a main house and a poolside restaurant where your aunt lives.'

'It sounds just about perfect,' said Andrina, managing to

avoid his outstretched hand as she leapt ashore because
she was quite sure she didn't need help. 'I can't wait to see
it!'

She plunged along the narrow jetty only to stumble
ignominiously on a loose plank. Two strong hands lifted
her easily and she found herself gasping against Ward
Prentice's chest.

'I should have warned you about the boards,' he said
with faint amusement. 'Everything at Castaways is a bit out
of control.'

She stood looking up at him in the faint light for a
moment before she thrust herself away.

'Thank you,' she said. 'I'll try to remember.'

They walked over the smooth coral sand where it was
still damp from the tide and then across the soft powdering
of dry beach where the water hadn't reached. Here tall
palms slanted crazily across the darkening sky and the
whole magic of the tropic night seemed to engulf them. It
was breath-stopping and a little alarming, Andrina thought,
following her guide into the thick growth of trees beyond
the palms, and then suddenly Castaways lay before them in
a small clearing bounded by rocks. The ground rose gradually from a semi-circular lawn to the perimeter of her
aunt's tropical garden where several palm-thatched cottages nestled among banks of hibiscus and oleander and
jasmine, their exotic blooms giving off a distinctive perfume
in the cool night air.

The approach to the house was over the rough grass of
the clearing by large stepping-stones which ended at a
broad verandah lit by several kerosine lanterns and two
large hanging lamps. A dozen or so glass-topped tables and
some white reclining chairs clustered round a blue-tiled
swimming-pool, and a bamboo-thatched bar hid among
the gathering shadows, still unlit. The reflection of the
lamplight twinkled on a row of bottles ranged on a rack at
the back and high cane stools stood waiting in a row to accommodate the first of her aunt's guests to appear for

dinner. A large Alsatian dog got up out of the shadows to inspect them.

'Friends, Ben!' Ward Prentice announced. 'Where's your mistress?'

'Not here! Not here!' a peculiar falsetto voice returned from the shadows. 'Gone. Gone away——'

Andrina's heart lurched at the information.

'It's all right,' said Ward. 'You'll get used to the birds.'

Two huge cockatoos stood on a wooden perch in a round enclosure at the end of the verandah, handsome, crested birds with bright-ringed, beady eyes which inspected them carefully, the birds heads on one side. Their plumage was a vivid green, their long tails hanging down almost to the bottom of their perch as they shuffled along, peering at the dog. A smaller grey-and-coral parrot, the talkative one, looked anxiously from the shadows towards them.

'Hi, Joey!' Ward greeted him. 'You've got a visitor.'

About to greet Joey with a conventional gesture, Andrina became aware of a small woman standing beside an inner doorway. She was no more than five feet tall and she wore a vividly-coloured beach-robe which reached right down to her feet, covering most of her body with the exception of her two plump arms which were tanned to a rich, dark brown from constant exposure to the tropic sun.

'Drina!' she exclaimed, coming forward to meet her. 'At last!'

'Aunt Belle!' Andrina stooped to kiss the warm, smooth cheek, thinking that her aunt had shrunk alarmingly in the years between their last meeting and now, but probably it was only because she herself had grown up in the meantime. 'It's ages since we met. I should have come sooner.'

'I had a mind to ask you,' Isobel Speitz said, holding her close. 'Yes,' she added, 'you should have come long ago, but now you're here we must make the most of it.'

She spoke with a broad American accent although she looked totally English, with her blue eyes under straight, fair brows and her pink-and-white complexion which she had never exposed to the harsh rays of the tropic sun. Her hair, which had faded a little over the years, was piled in a near-gold coronet on her shapely head and her hands were well-formed and beautifully manicured as she held her niece by both arms to continue her inspection.

'You're like your mother,' she concluded before she turned to Ward Prentice waiting in the shadows.

'I suppose our launch broke down,' she said. 'It generally does. Thank you for bringing my niece safely to the island, Ward. You're generally around in an emergency.'

There was the faintest hint of reproach in her voice as he put the suitcase down on the rattan matting which covered the tiled floor.

'It was no trouble,' he said. 'I was coming across anyway.'

'It was slightly out of your way.' Again the lack of warmth. 'It means you'll have to put to sea and go round the Bluff if the wind is suitable.'

'There's next to none, but I have a reliable engine.' He looked about him. 'I may even spend the night in the cove,' he decided.

'You'll dine here, in that case,' said Belle. 'We haven't many guests.'

Andrina had the distinct impression that her aunt's invitation had been extended entirely out of courtesy because Ward Prentice had done her a service when the launch had stranded her on Grenada and she had been unable to get away.

'I'm very grateful,' she said, looking across the verandah where he stood. 'I'd rather be here than back in St George's wondering what was going to happene to me.'

'You would have survived,' he said. 'I won't stay,' he added, turning to Belle with a faint smile. 'You must have a lot to talk about which couldn't possibly include a stranger.'

'You'll please yourself,' said Belle, in no way disconcerted by his blunt refusal. 'You always do.'

'How well you know me!' he smiled. '*Au revoir* for now,

Miss Collington,' he acknowledged Andrina with a wry twist of his handsome mouth. 'I hope you'll be happy on Flambeau while you remain here.'

'He doesn't mean a word of it,' Belle said in exasperation as he strode off across the yellow grass towards the beach. 'Ward Prentice is a law unto himself, as you'll soon find out. He lives here, but we don't really mix. He's something of an enigma; rich as Croesus, but odd.'

'A recluse?'

'It's not quite the right word. Nettleton's is a show-piece, the kind of estate everyone would like to have, but it wasn't that way when they bought it five years ago.'

'They?' queried Andrina.

'Ward and his brother. Richard I liked,' Belle declared. 'He was outgoing and a lot of fun and Ward wasn't at Nettleton's in the beginning. Just Richard and that wife of his, who was a flibbertigibbet if ever I saw one!'

'Is she there now—at Nettleton's?'

'No. She died in New York and Richard went off, trying to forget her. But we're wasting a lot of time on things that don't really concern us.' Belle put a plump arm around her niece's shoulders. 'We rarely see Ward over on this side of the island and when we do sparks invariably fly. I don't hold with the way he lives at Nettleton's, for one thing, though heaven knows, I could be prejudiced!'

'You don't like him,' Andrina suggested, unduly chilled by her aunt's revelations.

'I wouldn't say that, exactly.' Belle considered her carefully. 'You could say I wasn't drawn to him immediately, the way I was to Gerry. You met him, of course. What do you think of him?'

Andrina hesitated.

'He was very concerned about the launch, about not being able to get me over here,' she said for want of a better recommendation.

'He would be,' Belle nodded. 'He's a good boy—a charmer, of course, but genuine deep down. I'm very fond of him.'

'And he of you, I'm sure.'

'Do you say?' Her aunt looked exceedingly pleased. 'I don't know how I would have gotten over Albert's death if it hadn't been for Gerry. He was like a son to me; never left my side for three whole months afterwards. Wasn't that good, now?'

'Very.' Andrina thought that she must have misjudged the exuberant Gerald. 'He sent a message to say he would be home tomorrow without fail.'

'He's real thoughtful.' Belle led the way across the verandah into the house. 'I must get our radio attended to,' she added. 'There hasn't been a bleep out of it in more than a week.'

The house had once been beautiful, with high, raftered ceilings and terra-cotta pantiles flooring the main rooms and wide windows overlooking a spacious garden with a frontage to the sea, but now a tangle of tropic growth reached almost to the door, festooning walls and terraces with flowering vines which threatened to take over completely. Splashes of vermilion hibiscus and exotic frangipani hung down from the roof, smothering everything in a shower of blossom, the heady scent penetrating the rooms on every side.

'Here we are!' Belle announced. 'I want you to make yourself at home, honey, because I want you to stay here, if you will. I need one of my own kith and kin beside me, and your mother and I were real close. We were more like sisters than sisters-in-law, and your father and my Albert got on well together. You must take your time to make up your mind, of course,' she added, 'but I would appreciate it if you were to say "yes". I feel I need someone of my own sex around the place to confide in now and then, so think about it, won't you? You could be happy here, Drina, as happy as I was all those years before Albert died.'

And your love went away for ever, Andrina thought with a sharp pain in her heart.

'I know how it is, Aunt Belle,' she said, 'but I never thought of staying for good.'

'Then think about it now,' said Belle Speitz. 'Think hard.'

They dined in the open-sided restaurant which looked out across the lawn to the sea. There were six guests in the hotel, a Doctor Harvey and his wife who was a semi-invalid and two girls in their early twenties from Scotland who seemed slightly at a loss in such exotic surroundings. The other two were obviously on their honeymoon and sat closely together, holding hands between courses, semi-oblivious to everyone else.

Mrs Speitz, who had reappeared in a long kaftan, swept round the tables hoping everyone had all they wanted and were genuinely enjoying their meal. The doctor's gaze followed her as she joined her niece at their table in the corner.

'I wish I could do something for Mrs Speitz,' he said. 'She ought not to be out here on her own.'

'The girl's a niece, or something of the kind,' his wife replied, toying with her grapefruit. 'Why not speak to her?'

'I may do just that,' the doctor agreed. 'Seems a sensible sort of girl, don't you think?'

'Pretty, too,' his wife mused, 'with all that lovely auburn hair and those dark eyes. She's had an unhappy experience, I would say—probably a love affair.'

'Your imagination will get the better of you one of these days, Dot,' he said fondly. 'She's here on a once-in-a-lifetime holiday, I believe, and it might make all the difference to her aunt.'

'What are you trying to say?' his wife asked anxiously. 'Do you think Mrs Speitz is ill?'

'I wouldn't go as far as that, and she hasn't asked my opinion,' the doctor answered, 'but I think she ought to rest more than she does at present. She must be coming up for sixty and this climate can play havoc with a woman of her age.' He shifted his position to look out towards the lagoon. 'Personally, I find it too blamed hot on occasion, even when I'm sitting under a palm waiting for a coconut to fall on my head!'

'Henry!' she protested. 'You *wanted* to come.'

He patted her hand.

'Of course, I did, and I'm enjoying myself in spite of the coconuts!' he assured her.

Andrina had a healthy appetite and she enjoyed her dinner. It was exciting to eat out under the stars with the scent of frangipani in her nostrils and a huge round moon shining down between the boles of the palms. Briefly she had met and talked with her aunt's guests when they had gathered round the swimming-pool beside the bar to drink rum punches and the heady Piña Coladas which seemed to be the ladies' favourite, but several times she had found herself thinking about the man who had brought her to the island. Gerald Fabian she would meet again, but Ward Prentice was the unknown quantity, the 'near recluse' whom her aunt had tried to dismiss as irrelevant to their scheme of things at Castaways.

Yet they lived near each other on the same small island and not much more than a stone's throw away across the shoulder of rock which Ward had called the Bluff.

Before she went to bed that night she walked to the water's edge to look at it, finding it black and threatening even in the moonlight. The distant headland stretched from Tamarind Cove round the northern end of Flambeau, rising to two conical peaks in the interior before it sloped away to the east and south, a formidable barrier between the two estates. One day she might climb over the ridge to the far side of the island, but for the present it was almost forbidden territory. Ward Prentice had made it his home and he had not invited her there.

She turned to make her way back to the hotel where the glow-worm lights were strung out hospitably among the trees. Ward Prentice! Ward Prentice. What had she to do with a man like that?

CHAPTER TWO

THE rough sound of an engine shattered the peace of the lagoon early the following morning as the launch returned and began to discharge its stores. Native women who seemed to have appeared from nowhere ran out across the grass to help with the unloading, carrying the boxes on their heads with unconscious grace as they filed back across the flagstones with their considerable burdens. Backwards and forwards they went, like a string of busy ants, not stopping till the landing-stage was cleared.

Andrina, who had slept late, watched them from the patio of her bedroom where she had breakfasted on fresh fruit and delicious coffee brought to her by a smiling Carib girl who said her name was Francine. The leisurely pace of the island was already taking possession of her. There was no longer any hurry to do this or that while the sun shone in an incredibly blue sky and somewhere near at hand a bird was singing. Lovely, lovely island, she thought, full of sunshine and peace!

Beyond the patio the garden was aflame with colour, bougainvillea and hibiscus and frangipani tumbling in exotic bloom over the hidden terraces and pergolas, while delicate cream and mauve orchids sprayed out from the vines to add their fragile beauty to the scene. Andrina picked one of them as she passed on her way to the open-sided restaurant, tucking it into her belt as she reached the freshwater pool where most of her aunt's guests were already gathered. The doctor and his wife were resting on two of the cane reclining chairs with their eyes closed; the two girls from Scotland were already swimming in the pool, and the honeymoon couple were deep in conversation under the palms.

'Mrs Speitz, she in de bar,' one of the white-coated

waiters told her with an expansive smile. 'She rise ver' early in de mornin'.'

Andrina found her aunt seated in a cane chair at the end of the terrace, sheltered from the sun by the thick growth of an enormous vine which trailed sprays of white blossom to the terra-cotta tiles at her feet. As an extra precaution her head was covered by a large rattan sun-hat, frayed at the edges and bound by a chiffon scarf which matched one of the colours in the loose cotton kaftan she wore over a bathing-suit of the same colour.

'Come and sit beside me,' she commanded, pulling over a blue canvas chair. 'We have a lot to talk about.'

She laid aside her embroidery frame, stabbing her needle into the design which was only half complete.

'It's lovely,' said Andrina, taking it up. 'The colours are just perfect. Do you sew a lot?'

'All the time. I find it most relaxing, and I can also sell what I make. Nowadays, everything is for cash and it's surprising how eager people are to buy work they've seen in the process of completion. They fall over themselves to buy my screens because they can take them home and say "See where we've been". I must have embroidered Morgan and Captain Flint dozens of times,' she added, looking towards the two cockatoos drowsing on their high perch behind the wire screen of their circular cage. 'Joey isn't colourful enough,' she decided as the grey parrot hobbled towards them with his head on one side. 'Besides, he'll never keep still for more than a minute. Will you, Jo?'

The parrot screeched his agreement, fixed Andrina with a beady eye, and walked back along the terrace to the bar muttering: 'Where's Pete? He's late! He's late!'

Belle Speitz laughed.

'He's very fond of Pete, probably because he tends the bar! Gerry brought the launch over this morning, by the way, but I expect you heard the clatter. It seems to be all right, and he also has a new part for the radio receiver which should keep us in contact with civilisation for the next few months until something else happens to it. We've been unlucky with the launch, but everything wears out in time, I guess.'

Glancing through the dense greenery, Andrina became aware of a dilapidation which she hadn't noticed the evening before. In the harsher light of day Castaways looked almost shabby, with a chair here and there in need of attention and a broken table at her aunt's elbow which could have been mended or at least moved to a less conspicuous place. The swimming-pool, however, was sparkingly clean, its blue tiles matched by the hyacinth blue of a trailing vine above their heads. There were blue linen cloths on the bamboo tables in the restaurant and bowls of vivid hibiscus filled the alcoves in the main wall of the house where Francine was busy arranging tiny baskets of orchids as centrepieces for the lunchtime tables. In the evening each table was illuminated by fat little orange-coloured candles in glass bowls and there were taller candles in wrought-iron candelabra on the serving tables along the wall. Her aunt was doing her best to keep up the tone of Castaways, but nature was taking its inevitable toll. Soon there would be major repairs to be done, and Belle did not seem to be able to cope with the minor ones.

Before she could make any further assessment of the situation into which she had stumbled, Gerald Fabian made his appearance from the direction of the landing-stage carrying a net of vegetables over his shoulder. He had shaved, but he still had the look of a youthful beachcomber about him, his fair hair dishevelled, his faded jeans rolled to the knees, his shirt open to his waist while he carried his deck shoes slung by their laces about his neck.

'Greetings, family!' He deposited the net on the nearest chair and sat down, cross-legged, on the red-tiled floor at his employer's feet. 'Sorry about the launch,' he apologised. 'These things happen to me, and I'd been looking forward to bringing Andrina across. Never mind,' he concluded, 'things have worked out, though I had to entrust her to *Sea Hawk*, after all.'

'She got here safe and sound, as you see.' Belle was look-

ing at him closely. 'I thought you might have decided to
stay on Grenada for a few days.'

'There was no point,' he said, 'when I knew you needed
me over here. I bought the wine,' he added, 'and a few
extras which will come with the bill.' He stretched his
bronzed legs out to their full length. 'I'm glad to be back,'
he said.

'And you're bound to be hungry,' Belle suggested. 'I've
a fair notion you haven't eaten properly since you left here.'

'Francine will get me something,' he said indifferently,
'but I do need a wash.' He inspected his soiled hands with a
wry smile. 'There's nothing like working on an engine to
make you feel grubby.' He touched Belle on the shoulder.
'Don't bother to get up,' he said. 'I'll see to everything.'

He sauntered off in the direction of the kitchen, tweak-
ing the parrot's tail as he passed the bar.

'Saucy!' Joey remarked. 'Get off with you, man!'

Belle laughed.

'I don't know what I would do without Gerry,' she said.
'He's been here for so long.'

'How long?' Andrina was still watching Gerald Fabian's
progress among the shadows, seeing him stop beside
Francine, who was still arranging her posies in the restaurant, and noticing how he put his arm about the Carib girl's
waist as they disappeared through the slatted doors into
the kitchen. 'He seems to be—very familiar with the staff.'

'Oh, that's just Gerry's way,' Belle defended her manager. 'It doesn't mean a thing. They all adore him, and Pete
would lay down his life for him if he was asked. Josh, too;
they follow him everywhere.'

'He told me he was "Mr Fabian's right-hand man"!'
Andrina smiled. 'It's nice to know you have a contented
household.'

'I couldn't manage otherwise,' her aunt confessed. 'Your
uncle and I never had "words" in all the time we were together. Differences of opinion, yes, but friction just isn't
my thing. I've been plagued by rheumatism or something,
and haven't been able to do so much around the kitchen for

the past few years. Not as much as I used to do, anyway, but the boys have all been well trained and most of them are capable servants. They're happy in their work and they have an assured income, which they appreciate. If they didn't work for me at Castaways they would mostly spend their time beachcombing, and that's demoralising, to say the least of it. These islands are full of youngsters with very little to do, but I'm glad to say they don't resort to begging. If they try to make a few dollars they find something to sell, even although it's no more than a conch shell or a coconut carved to resemble an old man with a beard.'

Gerald came back to say that he had eaten and was duly satisfied.

'I'll fix up the radio as soon as I get the stores in. We could have some rain later in the day.' The green eyes searched their faces as if he wondered what they had been discussing. 'Did Prentice come ashore?' he asked.

'For a couple of minutes,' Belle told him. 'Just long enough to set down Drina's luggage and bolt back to *Sea Hawk*. Never even had a drink, but I suppose he had plenty on the schooner if he had a party on board.'

'He was on his own,' said Andrina. 'There was a second deck-hand, but that was all.'

'He's becoming more of a recluse than ever.' There was genuine dislike in Gerry's voice. 'He offered to help. I certainly wouldn't have asked.'

'We can't be too independent,' Belle pointed out. 'I would have worried if there'd been no word by ten o'clock. Living on an island has its disadvantages when your radio is out of order.'

'I'll see to it,' Gerry promised. 'Give me time.'

'What does Ward Prentice do on the other side of the island?' Andrina asked.

'Everything.' Gerry's tone was dry. 'Nettleton's is a model estate where he grows grapefruit and spices and bananas. He has also an interest in the fishing village down on the shore. A finger in every pie, in fact. You name it,

he's done it! That's why he wants our land. The whole
island—no more, no less.'

Belle Speitz shifted her position in the wide cane chair.
She was frowning and Andrina supposed that she shared
her manager's opinion of their neighbour, but surely Ward
Prentice had no designs on Castaways. It didn't seem to be
the sort of place he would covet, although he could want
the land to cultivate, adding it eventually to the Nettleton
estate.

'The island's divided practically down the middle,' her
aunt told her. 'On this side we have all the best beaches,
though some people like the east coast. It's wilder, but the
sands are black. You have to see L'Anse Deux Feux to appreciate what I mean. It lies at the foot of the mountain
which seems to dominate our island. You would see it on
your way in last night. There are really two peaks—hence
L'Anse Deux Feux, the beach between two fires, more or
less. The mountain, of course, is volcanic.'

'It sounds well worth a visit,' said Andrina, stretching
her legs in the sun.

'You'd be trespassing,' Gerry informed her. 'It's Nettleton territory and Prentice makes no bones about it.'

'Don't be absurd, Gerry!' Belle protested, the frown between her brows again. 'Ward doesn't exactly *encourage*
visitors, but he wouldn't forbid Andrina to go there. It's a
difficult road.' She turned to pick up her embroidery frame,
'but you could take the mini-moke. You drive, don't you?'

Andrina nodded, although she felt that she might be
lucky if the mini-moke got over the wild mountain road
without difficulty.

'I thought I might be able to walk,' she suggested.

'Walk?' The word seemed to horrify her aunt. 'You
wouldn't get very far in this climate before you were exhausted, honey. No, you must let Gerry take you when you
want to explore. He has plenty of time.'

'All the time in the world,' her manager agreed, 'but I
think you should restrict your activities to the lagoon at
first. You can swim all day there and dry off under the

palms, and if you're really the energetic type I'll take you snorkelling and sailing out in the bay.'

It was a promise he kept during the next two days, and Andrina revelled in the freedom of Castaways, helping where she could in the hotel and swimming in the crystal-clear waters of the lagoon. She made friends with Alison and Rita, the two Scottish girls, and joined the doctor and his wife for drinks round the freshwater pool when the sun went down. Once or twice she was aware of Doctor Harvey looking at her speculatively, but there was no confidence between them. Mrs Harvey remarked from time to time that Belle looked tired, but that was all.

On the third day she felt that she must stretch her legs a little.

'In spite of Gerry's warning, I'm going to walk,' she announced when the breakfast trays had been stacked away. 'He's going to be busy today testing the radio, so I thought I'd go over the Bluff. There's a road, I gather, and quite a lot of splendid scenery.'

Her aunt looked up from her embroidery.

'Take a hat,' she advised. 'And the road isn't that good after you reach the top. I don't know why you want to go walking, but I suppose it's one way of seeing the island.'

'The best way, I imagine.' Andrina kissed her on the cheek. 'You're sure there's nothing else I can do?'

'Quite sure, honey,' Belle smiled. 'I don't want you to feel you have to work all the time. It was your companionship I wanted.'

'And I'm running away!'

'Not too far, I hope. Maybe you'd better take the dog,' she added. 'He's badly in need of exercise. Hey, Ben!' she called to the drowsy Alsatian. 'Off you go for a nice long walk. You're as fat as butter, just sitting there!'

The Alsatian opened one eye.

'Come on, Ben, don't be lazy!' Andrina encouraged him. 'It won't be half as bad as you think!'

'Don't forget what I said about the road,' her aunt admonished. 'It's not good.'

Almost as soon as she had left Castaways behind Andrina realised that her aunt's estimate of the road was on the generous side. It was hardly a road at all, winding upwards through a tangle of vegetation which shut out the sun until it was finally left behind and she reached a flat, arid stretch of rock and stunted trees running out towards the headland. Before her were the twin peaks of the mountain, and suddenly she was alarmingly aware of them. Had she come far enough, and what had made her come at all? What was she searching for?

She called to the dog, waiting till he came to heel.

'We ought to go back, Ben,' she said. 'It really isn't much of a road.'

Yet she walked on until the dirt road ended, determined not to look at the mountain any more. The track she had followed from Castaways joined a reasonably surfaced road running north and south and as she stood wondering which way to take Ben made the decision for her. He bounded ahead of her down the southern slope as if he knew the way and she followed him with an odd feeling of inevitability which was hard to explain. Had she come out with a definite purpose in mind, not just to explore in a general way as she had pretended? Her curiosity about Ward Prentice had brought her this far, but there was still time for her to retrace her steps and no harm done.

It was then that she heard the birds. A forest of trees stretched ahead of her, a regulated plantation marching downhill towards the ocean. Each tree appeared to have been carefully planted to form the boundary of an estate and she had no doubt that it was Nettleton's. This was good husbandry on a scientific scale, planned and well ordered, with bananas on the higher slopes and other trees growing below.

The birds were somewhere in between, in some natural aviary which she could not see from the road, but their twittering followed her as she walked, a wild serenade of the woods which seemed almost uncanny in that deserted place.

Farther on she came to the entrance to the estate. There was no formal boundary fence, just the banana plantation with the great bunches of fruit shrouded in blue plastic to preserve them from the myriad insects ready to pierce their skins, and then a break in the living green wall where a narrow roadway led off through the trees. A notice on a wooden board said, briefly, Nettleton's, and that was all.

Andrina looked at it for a moment before she moved on, wanting to run back now in case she would be discovered, but not turning back. Here and there on the lower hillsides there was an occasional sign of life. Little houses that were no more than huts with thatched roofs perched among the natural scrub with groups of women and children standing around the open doors, gazing down the road. She could see right into some of the houses and they were all neat and clean. The children, too, were well cared for, the older ones guarding the baby of the family with infinite care. They were probably the Carib people her aunt had spoken about, the people who had once owned all the surrounding land, but possession did not seem to worry them, for they looked content, waving back in a friendly way when she raised a tentative hand in salute.

The road went steeply down to the shore, a wilder shore than the one she had left at Castaways with the ocean churning into a strong white foam against the rocky bastion of the Bluff, spending itself at the foot of the mountain before it ran back, exhausted, into a wide, black-sanded bay.

Such was the contrast to the coral sands of Tamarind Cove that she gasped in astonishment. White sand, black sand! The mountain had spent itself in one huge volcanic convulsion many years ago and the sands of L'Anse Deux Feux was the result.

It was a fantastic sight, with huge breakers from the Atlantic tumbling in a white foam over the black-sanded bay, and Andrina stood for a moment contemplating it in genuine awe. She seemed to be quite alone in a world of frightening contrasts, in a vast, strange world that fascinated while it repelled her.

'Ben!' she called. 'Ben, let's go home.'

The Alsatian stood his ground and began to bark, but it was a full minute before she recognised the object of his aggression. Galloping along the sand from the far end of the bay she saw a figure on a horse—or was it a donkey? Too small for a horse, she decided, and the rider was no more than a child. There was a flash of red cotton shirt and bare knees on a saddleless back as the donkey streaked past and then—catastrophe! Bare heels dug into the animal's flank, but suddenly he had had enough. His forefeet went firmly into the black sand, his head went down, and the intrepid rider went over his flattened ears like an arrow from a bow. The spare little body turned a complete somersault in mid-air before it landed ignominiously on the wet sand several feet from the donkey's nose.

Andrina held her breath. The child was still lying there and she felt unable to move. The thought of death presented itself with numbing certainty for a moment before she ran down between the rocks that skirted the shore. Donkey and rider were lost to sight, but when she saw them again the child was on his feet. He stood facing the recalcitrant little animal with the rein over his head and his own heels dug into the sand, pulling with all his might.

'You stubborn ol' mule!' he cried. 'Move, I tell you. Move!' Tugging on the rein, he beat the reluctant donkey on the chest with a small, clenched fist. 'You'll never get nowhere if you jus' stand still. You hear me, mule? You hear what I say?'

Gasping with relief, Andrina laughed aloud as she jumped down on to the beach and the child whirled round to face her. He was small and thin and wiry, with a tangle of corn-coloured hair much in need of cutting and his expression was immediately hostile.

'Who are you?' he demanded. 'Are you from the hotel over at Tamarind?'

Looking into the vividly blue eyes Andrina was sharply

reminded of Ward Prentice. The child's gaze was fearless, even arrogant, and he did not seem to mind the blood which trickled from a cut on his brow.

'Are you laughing at me?' he demanded.

'Not *at* you,' Andrina said. 'It was the way you did that complete somersault over the donkey's head. It was really funny, you know, so I couldn't help laughing when I realised you weren't seriously hurt.'

He swept a small brown hand over his forehead, dismissing the cut.

'It's nothing,' he said. 'I'll wash it in the sea and it will soon go away.' The shrewd blue eyes were still considering her. 'Did you walk all the way from Tamarind?'

'Yes. It was very pleasant. I stopped occasionally, of course, to look at the Carib houses and listen to the birds,' Andrina admitted.

'They're mine,' he informed her proudly. 'Some of them come from far away, like the mynah birds who live in Malaya mostly.'

She didn't have to ask if he lived at Nettleton's. His remark about the bird sanctuary and the penetrating blue gaze confirmed it beyond a shadow of doubt. He was Ward Prentice's child.

'What's your name?' she asked, steadying her voice.

'Salty.' The blue eyes challenged hers. 'I've always been called that.'

He was perhaps six years old, she decided. Maybe a little older because it was difficult to judge exactly in the circumstances. Certainly he had been allowed to develop naturally, with no restriction placed on his adventurous way of life. He would ride and fish and wander about the plantations at will, brought up to believe that it would all be his one day. But what of his formal education? She could not deny the fact that he was well spoken and his manners beyond reproach, although when he harangued the donkey he had slipped easily into the vernacular and no doubt he could hold his own with the Carib boys, who looked meek enough.

'I'm glad to meet you, Salty,' she said, holding out her hand. 'Do you ever come to Tamarind Cove?'

'No.' He shook her solemnly by the hand. 'There's plenty to do here on the plantation and I go often to the village. Sometimes I'm allowed to go out with the fishermen and we bring back the catch to sell it. Other times I go on *Sea Hawk*, but not too often. You see, I've got a sail-boat of my own and I can take it all round the bay,' he added proudly.

'And you've got the donkey,' Andrina pointed out.

'Oh, him!' he scoffed. 'I only ride him 'cos I haven't got a horse. I'm too small for a horse yet and not strong enough,' he added ruefully.

'You'll grow,' Andrina consoled. 'It happens to us all!'

'I'm not very big for my age,' Salty murmured, obviously repeating an adult assessment, 'but I don't care. I can *do* things, like swimming underwater without a snorkel, an' climbing, an' water-skiing. It's all easy,' he boasted, 'when you know how.'

No doubt he had been taught all these things by Ward himself. They were so alike, so fearlessly assured, father and son in every sense of the word.

She swallowed hard. But why should she feel disappointed, even cheated? Ward Prentice was no more than a passing acquaintance and he must remain so.

The donkey, having proved his point that goading was no way to achieve results, abandoned his entrenched position in the sand and came towards them.

'I must teach him a lesson,' Salty explained, leaping easily on to his back. 'I must make him gallop to the end of the beach and back again. Then he'll know not to stop suddenly half way and pitch me over his head.'

'A little gentle discipline never comes amiss,' Andrina murmured. 'Goodbye, Salty! It was nice meeting you.'

In spite of his self-assurance the child watched her turn away with a hint of regret in his eys.

'Will you come again?' he asked.

Andrina hesitated.

'I may do. I'm not just a guest at Castaways. I've come to

help my aunt,' she explained.

Salty dug small, determined heels into the donkey's side. 'Watch me ride!' he shouted over the sound of the breakers. 'Watch me!'

The shrill young voice held an unconscious plea for companionship and Andrina turned to face the mountain with an odd uncertainty in her heart. A mother's influence was obviously lacking at Nettleton's, but perhaps Ward Prentice had taken matters into his own hands at an early stage, deciding to mould Salty in his own image right from the start.

Suddenly she was brought up short by the fact that Ward himself was standing on the path immediately ahead of her.

'I must be trespassing,' she acknowledged, looking into his challenging blue eyes, 'but I saw Salty down on the shore and went to say "Hullo" to him. He was having trouble with the donkey.' When he did not speak she added firmly: 'Your son is very like you, Mr Prentice. There could be no mistaking his identity.'

'My son?' He laughed, white teeth flashing. 'Salty is a girl!'

She stared at him, unbelieving.

'A girl?' she repeated. 'But——'

'I'm bringing her up wrongly? Wasn't that what you were about to say, Andrina?' He used her Christian name with an arrogance which confirmed the fact that he had little use for the conventions. 'She rides and swims and sails as fearlessly as any boy, and why not? This is her life, so she has to know how to take care of herself. One day she'll have to go to school—I realise that—but so far I've been able to educate her after my fashion and we are both content. She is not quite six years old, so the social graces mean very little to her. And now,' he added, dismissing her silent criticism, 'since you've come this far, would you like to see the rest of the estate?'

They had halted at the narrow side road above the notice-board announcing that they had reached the main entrance to Nettleton's, and she hesitated, not quite knowing what to think of his abrupt invitation and whether to accept it or not.

'I've been away for rather a long time,' she decided. 'My aunt knows where I've gone, of course, but she could be worried if I didn't turn up before tea time. It's quite a distance back to Castaways.'

'It can be shorter through the estate,' he said, 'but please yourself. I thought you might be in need of a cooling drink.'

'It's certainly my problem,' she agreed. 'What about Ben?'

He looked down at the dog with an indulgent smile.

'Ben's all right,' he said. 'He hasn't the energy to chase the wild fowl.'

They walked along the narrow dirt road in the shade of the bananas, stopping every now and then to admire a particularly splendid bunch.

'They have to be protected,' Ward explained the plastic covering, 'otherwise they would be unmarketable. One blemish and a whole hand is ruined as far as the exporters are concerned. When we have a shipment they're cut and washed in our own sheds, then packed into the Company boxes and ferried out on barges to the ship lying offshore. It's quite a scene and is generally done in the early hours of the morning or late at night, whatever the ship's schedule dictates. Everybody works on this side of Flambeau,' he added. 'We don't carry passengers.'

'It's the way it should be,' she agreed, flushing at his scarcely concealed criticism of life at Castaways, 'although some people might not want to make a lot of money.'

His strong jaw tightened.

'It irks me to see good land going to waste,' he said, his eagle gaze sweeping the horizon from the twin-peaked mountain to the sloping foothills running down to the shore. 'Anything will grow here provided the soil is cultivated.'

It was easy enough to see what he meant. As well as the leafy bananas the whole estate was thickly forested. Mahogany, calabash and cedar, ebony and satinwood spread their branches against the sky, and lower down the slope a magnificent avenue of jacaranda trees marched triumphantly towards the lovely old plantation house looking down across a deep ravine to the ocean. It was a house Andrina would always remember. Built out above a natural rock garden, it resembled the prow of a ship, and she wondered if that was why Ward Prentice had chosen it as his home.

They approached it through a beautiful garden full of subtropical flowers and trees where gardenias and passionflowers grew in abundance and a vine she had never seen before shed delicate jade-coloured blossoms on the sheltered turf of the well-kept lawn.

'Did you do all this?' she asked. 'It's a botanist's dream.'

He smiled at the term she had used.

'I'm no gardener,' he said. 'I take the broader vision. Mangoes and yams and papaya are more in my line.'

'Someone must have made your garden.' Once again she was conscious of the heady perfume of frangipani filling the still air about them. 'A long time ago,' she guessed.

'It was planned by the wife of the original owner,' he explained, 'and added to through the years. My sister-in-law took a great interest in it for a while.' He stood looking at the jade-vine for a moment. 'I find it difficult to understand how anyone could think as she did, yet desert a place in the end.'

The tension in the atmosphere was suddenly very strong, the silence in the tree-shaded garden suddenly oppressive.

'She died,' Andrina said awkwardly.

'Yes.'

The house stood above them, waiting.

'We can go in this way,' he said, climbing the semicircular steps to the level of the verandah which had been built out on stilts overlooking the ravine.

'I'm putting you to too much trouble,' she objected.

'I told you it was a short cut to Castaways. What will you drink?' he asked. 'Orange, grapefruit, passionfruit juice or the ubiquitous Piña Colada? I can offer you a choice.'

'A Piña Colada comes first to mind!'

Ward led the way through glass doors into a semi-circular room which had been shuttered against the afternoon sun and she was vaguely aware of comfortable chintz-covered armchairs and timber beams which had been lovingly carved over a centruy ago. Satinwood occasional tables reflected the stream of light from the window he had opened and bowls of cream-and-brown orchids studied their pale reflections in the polished surface as in a garden pool. It was a house held together by a woman's hand, although no woman came to greet them.

'You think it an odd atmosphere for a child to grow up in,' he guessed, mixing their drinks at an ebony cabinet in an alcove.

'In a way,' she was forced to admit. 'It may make it harder for her to make the break when she does go to school. At five and a half Salty is probably more advanced in some ways than the average English child while in other ways she could be lagging far behind. By the way, what *is* her proper name? It can't possibly be Salty.'

He smiled at the suggestion.

'It was what she made of Sally when she first began to speak and somehow it stuck. Sally-Ann Prentice was too big a mouthful for such a scrap of humanity, so we settled on Salty in the meantime.'

'And she's never grown out of the idea? Nicknames are difficult things to shake off. Did—her mother go along with "Salty"?'

His expression changed dramatically.

'I doubt if she minded very much,' he said, but that was all.

Andrina crossed to the open window, aware of an odd constriction in her throat.

'A child without a mother's influence is greatly handicapped,' she said. 'I feel sorry for Salty.'

'You needn't be,' he returned crisply. 'She has everything she could possibly want, I can assure you. And now, if you're ready, I'll take you through the garden to the west road where you'll be just above Castaways.'

She finished what remained of her drink, following him out through the verandah door with a vague feeling of reluctance, and for a moment they stood at the verandah rail looking down across the ravine to a gleam of surf breaking on the shore far below. Orchids and jasmine and myrtle in ordered profusion beneath them, flanked by huge bushes of hibiscus and oleander and bright gleams of gardenias and passionflowers—the lingering spell cast by this exotic garden was hard to define and the enigmatic stranger by her side was part of it. He had told her very little about himself, answering only her direct questions about the child, and now he seemed to be waiting for her to go.

Proudly she turned away.

'I'm wasting your time,' she suggested, and he did not contradict her.

On their way through the estate she was amazed by the prolific growth on every side. Bananas were ripening everywhere and there were whole groves of nutmeg in trim, shady ranks waiting to be picked. He explained about the mace, rubbing it free of the nut between his fingers for her to see.

'If you're interested,' he said unexpectedly, 'we have a sizeable drying plant on the estate and Garson will take you over it any time you wish. I believe he gets some of your aunt's guests from the hotel, although it's a little far for them to walk.'

He had relegated to his overseer a task which he could have undertaken himself, but she could not ask for privileges, even although she wasn't exactly one of her aunt's hotel guests.

'I don't mind walking,' she observed. 'I've thoroughly enjoyed my day.'

Ward didn't say 'Come again' as he might have done. In fact, his attitude was hardly one of encouragement at all, and when she held out her hand for the nutmeg he had picked he gave it to her with the faintest of smiles. In the moment when their fingers touched the contact was like a red-hot flame and she drew back instinctively.

'Don't you like them?' he asked.

'Of course! And thank you very much for them—and the drink.'

She hurried away without looking at him again, unaware that he stood for several minutes at the merging road ends, wondering about her.

Before she reached the brow of the hill which led down to Castaways she knew that she was being followed, and the lazy clip-clop of hooves convinced her that Salty must be somewhere in the vicinity. She waited for the donkey and rider as they came round a bend in the road.

'Hullo!' said Salty as if they had parted several days ago. 'I wondered if I would see you again.'

'Here I am!' Andrina smiled. 'I've been to Nettleton's since we met on the beach.'

Salty frowned.

'I saw you walking back,' she said. 'Did you go into the house?'

'Yes. We had a drink on the verandah. It was very warm.'

'Did you see the birds?'

'Some of them. I certainly *heard* them!'

'My father collected them from all over the world.' Salty paused thoughtfully. 'He wanted me to know about birds, I guess.'

'It's very nice to have such a handsome aviary,' said Andrina, 'and probably you'll add to it as you grow older.'

'Mrs Speitz has a parrot and two cockatoos. I wish I could come and see them,' Salty mused.

'We would love to have you, and Joey could learn your name,' Andrina suggested. 'He's quite bright at picking up new names.'

'What I would like best is to swim in your lagoon,' Salty confessed. 'It's often too rough on our side of the island and the sand is black. I don't like black sand. It looks dirty, though it's really quite clean. You see,' she added, 'it's the volcano that makes it black.'

She had spoken in a stage whisper, as if she feared the mountain, and Andrina hurried to reassure her.

'I'm quite certain you'd be made welcome at Castaways. Why not come one afternoon and see for yourself?'

The child hesitated. 'I'd have to ask permission first, even though I'm five—and a bit,' she decided. 'Do you have to ask when you want to do anything exciting?'

'I did when I was your age.' Andrina looked up at the tiny figure on the donkey's back. 'I'm sure you'll be able to come,' she said.

Salty heaved a deep sigh.

'I'll do my best,' she said politely. 'I'm not supposed to sail round the Bluff, but I could ride across on Pedro.' She drew the rein tight, turning the donkey's head towards Nettleton's. 'I could come in the morning when it's not so hot.'

Wondering what the child did with herself all day when it was too hot for riding on the sun-baked roads of the Bluff, Andrina set off for Tamarind Cove with the Alsatian at her heels. Ben had enjoyed a surreptitious doze in the shade of a tamarisk bush while Salty had engaged her in conversation and now he trotted briskly ahead of her on the downhill path, satisfied that his enforced exercise was almost at an end. In places the narrow, twisting dust road was almost obscured by the jungle growth of trees and vines which grew on either side, but here and there a wild banana tree with its miniature fruit and a scarred grapefruit tree suggested that the land behind Castaways might once have been cultivated. Ward Prentice had said that it was a waste of good soil to allow it to run to jungle and she felt half inclined to agree with him. Yet what could her aunt really do about it? She was a woman on her own; an elderly woman now who preferred to sit in the sun and embroider exotic flowers on to canvas for her own pleasure and her guests' delight.

Gerald Fabian came to meet her, his brows drawn in a frown.

'Where on earth have you been?' he asked.

'Walking.'

'I know that, but you must have gone quite a long way. I told you how exhausting it would be.'

'I didn't climb the mountain, if that's what you're suggesting,' Andrina laughed. 'I—just sort of went on and on till I came to the other side.'

'You went to L'Anse Deux Feux?' he asked sharply. 'Did you meet anyone?'

'Ward Prentice and Salty. She's quite a girl!'

'She's a spoiled brat, by anyone's calculation,' he said, 'and Prentice wouldn't appreciate your visit if you went to the house.'

'I didn't go uninvited.' She walked steadily ahead of him towards the hotel. 'He offered me a drink, probably because he saw how warm I was. I don't think you're altogether right about him, Gerry. He isn't an ogre, and we can't blame him for wanting privacy on his own estate. He mentioned that our guests were welcome to go to the packing sheds, either to see the bananas being washed or the spices dried.' She felt the nutmeg Ward had stripped of its mace for her warm in her hand. 'In no way does he appear to be an absolute recluse.'

'He's certainly impressed you,' Gerry said distantly, 'but I'd watch out for Mr Ward Prentice, if I were you. At one time he had rather an unsavoury reputation around these parts—and he's certainly had his women friends. Quite a few of them,' he added darkly, 'and most of them aboard *Sea Hawk*.'

'It doesn't really concern me very much,' Andrina tried to say convincingly. 'I'm not exactly in his class.'

He laughed heartily.

'You underestimate yourself. A man like Prentice soon gets bored with the sophisticated type, and you're new.' Swiftly he put his arm about her waist. 'I'm glad you've come, Drina,' he said, using the abbreviated form of her name which her aunt preferred. 'We can be good friends, you and I. Even more than that,' he suggested, drawing her nearer. 'Your aunt needs you on Flambeau. She wants you to stay.'

Andrina found it difficult to walk on in what was more or less a close embrace.

'I haven't made up my mind about staying,' she said, attempting to free herself. 'And if we don't hurry we're going to be late.'

Suddenly he bent to kiss her on the cheek, but she turned her head to avoid his lips.

'Drina,' he murmured into her hair, 'you're the most exciting thing that's happened to Castaways for a long time. We could do so much together and your aunt would nod her approval. It would be her chance to sit back and relax. Ever since Albert Speitz died she's been worried about the future, not sure whether to let the hotel go or not, and recently——'

'Yes?' she asked sharply.

'Oh, it's nothing to worry about,' he assured her. 'She's just slowed down a bit, not been quite the competent old girl she used to be when they first came here.'

She turned to face him.

'Gerry, are you trying to tell me she's ill—seriously ill?' He shook his head.

'Nothing like that. I guess she's just tired,' he said. 'She must be sixty, if she's a day.'

'I don't know her age. She was younger than my father, but sixty isn't considered old these days, is it?' A twinge of foreboding stirred in her heart. 'She hasn't said anything——'

'She wouldn't, and I could be wrong,' he agreed, 'but when she first decided to send for you she said she needed "her own kith and kin" around her. Sometimes that's significant.'

'It's also natural,' said Andrina as she increased her pace along the narrow road.

Soon they came to the clearing where Castaways dreamed in the sun, yet the suggestion of drowsy peace and contentment had been dispelled for her by Gerald Fabian's words. The scent of frangipani was still heavy on the air and her aunt still sat with her embroidery on her knee under the protective vine, but a small, insidious fear had crept into the peace of the garden, like the serpent in Eden, making her afraid.

Belle looked up at their approach, smiling her welcome.

'Gerry thought you'd gone for good,' she said. 'Did you climb to the top of the mountain?'

'I've reserved that for another day when I have more experience.' Andrina took the embroidery frame to inspect her aunt's progress. 'You haven't done a thing since I left!' she exclaimed in mock reprimand. 'You've been asleep!'

'Just dozing,' Belle admitted ruefully. 'I guess I must have nodded off after Gerry went in search of you. Did you go far?'

'As far as L'Anse Deux Feux,' Andrina informed her.

'And Nettleton's,' Gerry put in with a wary eye on his employer's face. 'She had the temerity to beard Ward Prentice in his den.'

They laughed, but presently Mrs Speitz said more seriously:

'Did you go to the house?'

Andrina nodded.

'What's it like these days?' Belle asked curiously. 'A man's place?'

'Not in the way you mean. It seemed to be well enough looked after—dusted and polished—and there were fresh flowers in the vases, but I suppose you could call it a man's domain, if you wanted to.'

'It's no place for a growing child,' her aunt returned with unexpected vehemence, 'and a girl at that!'

'I did think Salty was a boy at first,' Andrina had to admit. 'She was riding a donkey bareback along the sands as if there was no tomorrow!'

'That's exactly what I mean,' said Belle. 'She's completely undisciplined and half the time she's alone with the servants, apparently. When I used to go up there with the hotel guests we often came across her riding in among the spice trees, but she never seemed very eager for our company.'

'She'd like to come to Castaways now,' Andrina told

her, 'to swim in the lagoon and look at the coral. She has a sail-boat of her own, but she's been forbidden to come round the Bluff in it.'

'I should think so!' her aunt exclaimed. 'She must be no more than five years old.'

'Five-and-a-bit!' Andrina smiled, remembering Salty's insistence on the bit.

'What's Ward doing about her schooling, in that case?' Belle asked indignantly. 'She's growing into a savage and he appears to be doing nothing about it.'

'I don't think anyone could persuade him that what he's doing is wrong,' Andrina said thoughtfully. 'Salty seems to enjoy herself, up to a point, and it's a life that would appeal to most children—free and uninhibited.'

'In the States she would be going to school in a few months' time; in England she would already be there,' her aunt pointed out.

'She may have a governess,' Andrina suggested. 'Someone to teach her in a general way.'

'Did you see anyone like that?'

'No,' Andrina was forced to admit, 'but the house looked lived-in. There was what you might call a woman's touch about everything.'

'He has a housekeeper of sorts going in from the village —one of the fishermen's wives,' her aunt observed, 'but he would be better served with someone like Luella, for instance, who's been trained in Barbados.'

'I didn't get as far as the village.' Deliberately Andrina switched the subject away from Nettleton's. 'How far is it?'

'Too far for you to go on foot and unaccompanied,' her aunt decided. 'Gerry will take you in the Moke one of these days.' And with that she went indoors.

Gerald Fabian had been listening to their conversation without taking part in it and Andrina felt that he was displeased by the way her visit to L'Anse Deux Feux had turned out. Yet he had no claim on her, she thought, no priority right to her company even although he was the pleasant companion she had thought about when she had first come to the island. Easy-going and humorous, he made her laugh when otherwise she might have felt sad. He was the sort of person who might take her future in his hands and make a happy thing of it if only she could thrust the past away.

'What can I tempt you to?' he asked, picking up one of the lunch menus as they went through to the restaurant. 'Melon or flying-fish——'

'I couldn't bear to eat flying-fish!' Andrina exclaimed. 'Not after watching them on the way over on *Sea Hawk*.'

'You'll change your mind once you've tasted them,' he said callously, 'but melon it will have to be in the meantime. Then you ought to try one of your aunt's island specialities. She's built up quite a cullinary reputation in these parts, as a matter of fact. She used to do most of the cooking herself, but now she supervises. Luella is her willing slave in the kitchen and the boys are all mesmerised by her talent. Your aunt is a very special lady, and no mistake!'

'How long have you known her?' Andrina asked.

'Oh—off and on for about six years.'

'She's very fond of you.'

'I'm glad.' A deep satisfaction lit his eyes for a moment. 'And of course I'm concerned about her.'

'Do you think I should speak to Doctor Harvey?' asked Andrina.

He hesitated.

'There's really nothing specific to tell him,' he decided, pulling out a chair for her at the table they occupied in a corner overlooking the beach.

Andrina sat down facing him, her thoughts still taken up with her aunt's affairs.

'I wonder if she'll ever leave here,' she said half to herself.

'Not if you decide to stay.'

'Why do you feel so sure? She's only known me for a short time.'

'Blood is thicker than water,' Gerry pointed out.

'I suppose so.'

He sat down, his long legs thrust out under the wicker table.

'Why Andrina?' he asked curiously. 'It's an unusual name.'

'I was called after my grandfather—Andrew Milton.'

'Ah, I see! No boy in the family?'

'Only me. My mother was very fond of her father. If I'd been a boy I would have been just Andrew and no complications,' Andrina said. 'Truth to tell, I'm not very fond of my name, as such.'

'But you were fond of your grandfather?'

'Very.' She gave her order to the waiter. 'No flying-fish,' she said firmly.

'Flyin'-fish, they ver' good,' he beamed. 'Mr Gerry, he eat them all de time!'

'Not this time,' Gerry laughed. 'I'll have grapefruit for a change.'

Andrina looked round for her aunt.

'She's having hers on a tray in her room,' Gerry explained.

Andrina half rose from the table.

'Then she *is* ill!'

'Not necessarily. She often eats on her own patio while the guests congregate round the bar. That way she can take the dog and the parrot for an afternoon nap when most of the guests go down to the beach to snooze their life away or just idle in the boats to look at the coral. I'll take you in a glass-bottomed boat,' he offered. 'Unless you would rather snorkel?'

'Either way,' Andrina agreed. 'Perhaps I'd better try the boat first.'

'You'll feel freer when you swim around,' he told her. 'You can go from place to place at will. Come to think of it,' he added, his blue gaze narrowing on the horizon, 'it's a bit like life. When you move from place to place you're free from entanglements. There's nothing to trap you.'

Andrina considered him lazily.

'Is that how you feel, Gerry?' she asked.

'It's how I *felt* until quite recently.'

'What made you change your mind?'

He shrugged.

'Advancing years,' he grinned, 'and a suggestion of root-lessness.'

She gazed out over the turquoise water.

'Is this what you really want?' she asked. 'Helping to run a remote hotel on a Caribbean island?'

'What could be more idyllic?' he countered without actually answering her question. 'Time I settled down, I suppose. Or so your aunt tells me. I'll be thirty in September.'

'With little to show for it, do you mean?'

His handsome mouth tightened.

'Years of contentment,' he suggested. 'That ought to mean something. What about you?'

'I've—never thought very much about contentment,' she admitted. 'One accepts it when it's linked with happiness, I suppose.'

'And when the bad moments come?' Gerry fingered his wineglass, turning it slowly on the straw place-mat.

'I came here to forget them,' she confessed, her eyes clouding at the memory of her first love.

He leaned towards her across the table.

'Do you want to tell me?' he asked. 'I can always lend a sympathetic ear.'

She looked into his questioning eyes.

'It's quite simple,' she said. 'I fell in love, and he married someone else. Someone with a great deal of money, in fact. It was a shock, but I think I'm over it now.'

His hand covered hers on the highly-polished table.

'I hope so,' he said. 'No use crying over spilt milk, is there? When you've been here for a few weeks you'll see what I mean. You learn to relax, mentally as well as physically.'

'In other words, I won't think too deeply,' Andrina smiled.

'I wouldn't say that.' He waited for their main course to be set before them. 'You learn to take things as they come. You don't challenge fate any more.'

'It's a negative sort of approach.'

'Maybe, but it's the way things are,' he said. 'Out here, anyway.' He watched the erratic flight of a yellow bird beneath the rafters. 'It's the natural effect of sunshine and warmth—the lotus-eating way of life, and very few people can resist it.'

Andrina thought of Ward Prentice who had slashed his way through the jungle to improve Nettleton's, but perhaps he had an incentive, something to make work worth while.

'I'm not going to accept your philosophy till I've tried it out,' she laughed as the waiter brought their coffee to the table. 'What are you going to do this afternoon?'

'Take you coral-watching. It's all part of the service,' Gerry declared. 'Get into a swim-suit and take a hat or a scarf for your head. You have to lie flat in the boat.'

His plan had been to take her alone, but in the end the two Scottish girls joined them, so eager to view the reef from the comparative safety of a boat that he could not refuse them.

It was certainly an idyllic situation as they took it in turns to lie flat on the bottom of the boat looking down into an underwater paradise alive with darting fish and swaying seaweed with the multi-coloured coral forming turrets and palaces and fantastic caves where a hidden monster could so easily be lurking among the shadows quite unknown to them.

The sun was well down in the west before Gerald turned the boat towards the shore.

'Time to go back,' he declared. 'There's a wind coming up.'

They sat in the boat, smiling at one another, utterly satisfied with their adventure. On the far side of the reef a white sail marked the passage of a yacht bound for one of the other islands of Union or Cannounan or Mustique, which were no more than faint smudges on the horizon. The whole sky was devoid of cloud, but when Andrina turned to look at Flambeau a faint haze hung down over the mountain, suggesting rain.

Narrowing her eyes, she made out the faint shape of a child on a donkey riding across the Bluff, riding away from a high vantage-point from which she would be able to overlook Tamarind Cove and Castaways.

Curiously disturbed by the sense of loneliness suggested by the distant figure, she wondered if Salty had visited the hotel in their absence only to be disappointed at not finding them there.

They helped Gerald to pull the boat up the beach to the safety of the palms where it would remain overnight.

'That was wonderful!' one of the girls exclaimed appreciatively as they gathered sandals and towels together for their short walk to the hotel. 'I never imagined it would be so—breathtaking.'

Andrina walked slowly across the soft white sand, her toes sinking deeply into its warmth, her heart suddenly as light as air. This, surely, was contentment, a dismissal of heartache and memory, a freedom of the spirit which banished time!

Before they had reached the sun-baked lawn they were aware of chaos. A great commotion had disrupted the peace of Castaways. Joey, the parrot, was chattering at the top of his voice, the cockatoos were screeching as they shuffled along their perch, and Ben was adding to the general hullabaloo by voicing his own protest in a deep, resonant howl.

'Something's happened!' Andrina cried, running across the stepping-stones. 'Something serious——'

Doctor Harvey met her at the edge of the verandah.

'My aunt?' she gasped. 'What's happened?'

He took her by the arm, leading her to a chair beside the swimming-pool.

'It's nothing,' he said. 'Nothing to get unduly alarmed about this time.'

'This time?' she repeated. 'What do you mean?'

'Your aunt passed out. She was sitting in the sun talking to my wife a few minutes ago. It's not serious, but I've been meaning to have a word with you. I've told her that she ought to see a specialist.'

Andrina's heart contracted at the news.

'Why?'

'She has this heart condition. Had it for some time, I should say, and disregarded it because there was no one to confide in, perhaps.'

'There is now,' Andrina said firmly. 'Where is she?'

'In her own room.' The sad, kind eyes were suddenly apologetic. 'I may have alarmed you unnecessarily.'

He followed her through the red-tiled courtyard to the shade of the colonnaded passage which led to the bedrooms, most of which were unoccupied at that time of day, and before they had reached the end door Andrina heard her aunt's voice raised in protest.

'This is ridiculous! I've never been ill in my life,' Belle was declaring. 'It was the sun, sitting in it for too long.'

Andrina passed Mrs Harvey in the doorway, going straight to the bed where Belle Speitz lay propped up by pillows, her vivid eyes full of protest, her face white as the pillows themselves.

'You'll have to tell them not to fuss,' she said as soon as she saw her niece. 'I'm all right, or I will be once I've had a cup of tea.'

Doctor Harvey felt for her pulse.

'You're not too bad,' he said, sitting down on the edge of the bed, 'but you'll do better when you stop arguing. I've told you the prospects and you said you would take time to think about them. Have you done that?'

'He wants me to see a specialist,' Belle said to Andrina, completely ignoring the question, 'but that means Barbados.'

'I'll go with you,' Andrina offered immediately, but her aunt shook her head.

'Who'll look after the hotel?' she demanded. 'If I go I'll

go easier if I know you're in charge.'

'There's Gerry.'

Belle's eyes clouded.

'I've treated him like a son,' she said, 'ever since he came here. I'm very fond of him——'

'But——?'

'He's irresponsible.' Belle looked upset. 'Perhaps if he married someone suitable and settled down I'd feel happier. In some ways he's my responsibility because I persuaded him to stay in the first place.'

'Don't worry about Gerry, of all people,' Andrina said crisply. 'He can take care of himself. At the present moment the most important thing is getting you to Barbados.'

'I'll fix up a consultation,' Doctor Harvey offered. 'We'll be going back in the morning. I don't know how long it will be before I can get you an appointment, but I'm sure I can fix it without keeping you waiting too long. In the meantime, rest as much as you can and don't worry.' He patted her hand. 'Everything will work out.'

When he left with the two Scottish girls and the honeymoon couple in the morning the hotel would be empty, but already Andrina knew that Castaways was booked for the remainder of the season. Eight new guests were due and it was too late now to consider cancellations. They would already be in Barbados, waiting to join the Islands plane, and Gerry would pick them up in Grenada when he took the launch across later in the week. There was no question now about whether or not she should stay at Castaways. She was fully committed in this emergency, glad in an odd sort of way that the decision had finally been taken out of her hands.

'Don't worry about the hotel,' she said when her aunt looked up from the bed. 'I'll look after it.'

CHAPTER THREE

THE following morning Gerry brought the launch in from its moorings, tying it up against the wooden landing-stage where most of the luggage was already lined up in neat rows, suitcases and canvas grips and duffle-bags which had seen better days and some very new and shiny luggage which obviously belonged to the honeymoon couple. They had kept so much to themselves that Andrina felt she hardly knew them even after six days, but they thanked her shyly for a wonderful holiday before they took their seat in the well, waiting for the others to join them. Doctor Harvey had gone for a last quick look at her aunt and Belle had rewarded him with a confident smile.

'She'll be all right,' he assured Andrina when he came to the office to pay his bill. 'Just you see that she stays in bed for a day or two and doesn't sit in the sun when she's well enough to get up.'

Belle's immediate reaction to his advice was that she was well enough now, but she stayed in bed as she was told, nodding when Andrina said that everything was well under control.

'I don't know what I would have done without you,' she said before she fell asleep.

The remainder of the morning was a hectic rush of sheet-changing and rearranging rooms. Although she had no knowledge of catering, Andrina believed in the calm approach, taking her time from Luella and the shy little Carib girl who looked after the bedrooms. As the pile of discarded linen built up on the floor she listened to Luella singing in the kitchen, the soft, crooning Islands songs which had been passed down over the years from mother to daughter or father to son. Josh, too, had a fine voice which he used as he helped to polish glasses in the bar or fished leaves from the swimming-pool with a long, hooked pole.

The day was warm without being sultry, although Andrina was glad of the vines which sheltered her from the sun. So much of her work was out of doors because Castaways was open to the cooling trade winds on every side, but after a light lunch of fruit and salad she decided to walk along the beach in the opposite direction to the Bluff. Her aunt was comfortably settled for the afternoon and would probably drift into a refreshing sleep and the launch wouldn't return much before nightfall. She took a bathing suit and a towel in a bright yellow bag which matched her linen dress, discarding her sandals as soon as she reached the shore.

The white-sanded beach stretched out far ahead of her in a long curve with a background of trees reaching almost to the water's edge where she could sit in the shade to dream an hour away. At times she could hardly believe that she was here in this island paradise walking lazily along the shore with nothing but the prospect of swimming in the crystal-clear water ahead of her. There was no cloud in the sky above her head and only the singing of the surf like a mighty pulse-beat to complement the sighing of the palms. The spell cast by this exotic, enigmatic island was hard to resist, far harder than she realised.

Beyond the lagoon the beach began to narrow and soon she was almost at the end of it where the rocks rose steeply again to a little promontory which faced south and seemed to be the very end of the island. She had come a long way.

Selecting a patch of very white sand, she put the yellow beach-bag into the hollow made by the protruding roots of a coconut palm and began to undress. It was a wonderful sensation to feel the sun warm on her bare flesh and the prospect of a long swim out beyond the reef was more than pleasing. She slipped on her white suit to wade into the shallow green water, feeling its cooling touch against her limbs, and finally she spread her arms and began to swim. Beyond the reef it was almost as calm as it was at Castaways, but now there was a vast suggestion of space, of unlimited ocean stretching away to infinity, a whole new world of shining, sparkling sea which she longed to conquer and make her own.

Was this how Ward Prentice felt, she wondered, when he sailed off on *Sea Hawk* alone? Turning on her back to gaze up at the sky, she thought of him as the essential mariner, never so happy as when he went to sea. Would such a man ever stay on Flambeau for good?

Idly she allowed the tide to carry her along while she felt the gentle trade wind brushing her cheeks, passing like a sigh. She could just make out the curve of the island as it turned eastwards towards L'Anse Deux Feux and she thought that the village must be over there on the other side of the promontory. How big? A scatter of fishermen's huts with an adobe building housing a general store and a landing-stage probably no bigger than the one at Castaways. At this time of day the fishermen's nets would be drying in the sun, slung between the boles of the palms, and little boys would be searching for flotsam along the shore. It was a picture she had seen often enough on her way to the jetty on Grenada, one which had imprinted itself on her mind as the true island scene.

But now it was time to return. The sun was slanting into the sea behind her and the beach looked far away. She was a good swimmer, but she miscalculated the spot on the shore where she had undressed. Her yellow bag was nowhere to be seen.

This way or that? She decided that she had come ashore too far south and was about to enter the water again when a man stepped out of the shelter of the trees. She knew him immediately. Ward Prentice was coming towards her, carrying her yellow bag.

Standing quite still on the sun-warmed sand, she was once again fully aware of the magnetism of his strong personality and of a sudden new desire to run away. But where could she run to with the vast expanse of the Caribbean behind her and Ward diminishing the distance between them with every step? He was dressed in light cord breeches and a thin silk shirt open to the waist, and the sun glinted on highly-polished riding-boots and on the whip in his hand. He was no longer the pirate on board his black schooner, but this other image of him was even more disconcerting. Now he was the powerful overlord of a prosperous estate whose bounds he was determined to widen in every way he could.

She blinked at him in the penetrating sunlight, feeling hopelessly vulnerable as she stood there in her scanty swim-suit, fresh from the sea. Then, something about the half-smile in his lips goaded her to say:

'Am I trespassing again? I had no idea this end of the island was private property.'

'It does belong to Nettleton's, but there's no reason why you shouldn't use it,' he said. 'That wasn't why I brought your bag along.' He held it out to her. 'You're perfectly at liberty to leave it under the palms, but I wouldn't advise it. The natives are not thieves—far from it—but they have a natural curiosity and the boys, especially, like a piece of flotsam to carry back to the village. If you were out of sight, as you were to me at first, they wouldn't know what to do with your bag and might take it away to find its rightful owner.'

'Yes,' she admitted. 'How careless of me, but there didn't seem to be anyone in the whole wide world when I undressed and I never gave the bag a thought. It seemed perfectly safe to leave it when there was nobody about.'

'The boys are always about,' he told her. 'They have very little to do when they're not in school and they're naturally curious. You'll draw their attention wherever you go, I'm afraid, but don't let them pester you if you want to be alone. Tell them quite plainly and they'll drift away as quietly as they came. They're not scroungers, you see, and their manners are good. Don't buy anything from them if you don't want it. They are really quite proud and some of the shells they offer take a lot of finding. Even the coconuts have to be brought down from the trees!'

He stood looking at her, the penetrating blue gaze seeming to strip her of her meagre covering of white cotton, and

hastily she sought the towelling beach-jacket she had left in
the bag. He helped her on with it, his fingers touching the
sun-warmed flesh of her shoulders so that she drew the
jacket more firmly round her as he moved away.

'It's wonderful down here,' she observed hastily. 'Outside the reef, I mean. There's a certain freedom about the
open sea when you're a strong swimmer.'

'I thought you would prefer to be in the lagoon,' he said,
still looking down at her. 'It's safer when you don't have to
cope with the pull of the tide.'

His remark seemed to be an oblique attack on her ability
to deal with life, and she flushed angrily.

'I've never been particularly protected, even in England,'
she told him, 'and it shouldn't be too difficult for me here.
My aunt may have to go to Barbados for a few days—she
needs a specialist's advice—and I'll manage Castaways in
her absence. It shouldn't tax my powers of application,' she
smiled, 'with everything moving at such a leisurely pace.'

'Is your aunt ill?' he asked abruptly.

'Not seriously, I hope, but a doctor who's been a guest at
the hotel for the past fortnight thinks that she should have
a second opinion, and I heartily agree.'

'Will she give up if things go wrong?'

'No.' Her tone was curt. 'She loves Flambeau. It was
where she lived with her husband for so many happy years,
the happiest, most contented years of her life, I should
imagine.'

'When she sent for you did you intend to stay?'

'No.' She drew the towelling jacket more securely about
her shoulders, as if she felt a sudden chill. 'But I mean to
stay now, certainly for as long as my aunt needs me.'

She searched his face, prepared to see disappointment
there, but there was no immediate reaction to her decision.
Instead, he turned to the grove of palms where a magnificent red stallion was tethered, loosening the rein as if he
were about to ride away.

'Thank you for rescuing my beach bag,' Andrina said.
'I'll walk back along the road.'

'There's a path above the shore, high up,' he told her.
'Once you've climbed to the top you get a magnificent
view of the bays on the other side. I ride this way quite a
lot. It saves time.'

She hesitated.

'I suppose you were working,' she said, 'not just riding
out for pleasure.'

His teeth flashed in a quick smile.

'You've made up your mind about me very quickly,' he
said. 'Yes, I was working. It's easier to ride a horse around
Nettleton's than depend on a mini-moke. There are some
places that only a horse can go, and I like the exercise.'

She sat down on a palm root to put on her sandals.

'I half expected to see Salty,' she said.

'The donkey has difficulty in keeping up with Simon,'
he answered, drawing the rein over the stallion's head to
lead him, 'and she really must work occasionally. Contrary
to what you believe,' he added, 'I'm concerned about her
education. I know she leads an unorthodox sort of life, but
she thoroughly enjoys it. She's completely free to roam
about the estate at will.'

'You're bringing her up like a boy!' The words were out
before Andrina realised how critical they must sound. 'Does
your wife agree?'

A dark frown settled on his brow.

'I'm not married,' he said curtly.

Feeling that she had touched on a particularly sore spot,
she stood up to face him.

'If you were,' she said, 'you'd perhaps be able to see my
point of view about Salty. She isn't growing up naturally.
You're treating her like a boy and she's acting like one.'

Ward laughed her criticism aside, standing close to the
horse's head as she picked up the yellow bag.

'What would you have me do?' he asked with a dangerous glint in his eyes.

She hesitated, remembering how independent Salty had
tried to look as she rode off across the black volcanic sands
of L'Anse Deux Feux yet seeing, too, the lonely little figure

sitting astride the donkey as Salty had looked down towards the lagoon.

'Salty needs a home background,' she said involuntarily and without thinking of the obvious implication of her advice. 'A mother's influence, if you like.'

He drew a little nearer and her heart began to beat with alarming rapidity.

'You talk like a self-righteous schoolma'am,' he said. 'Is that what you are, or are you applying for the position of my wife?'

The vividly blue eyes were coldly amused now and she stood back, confused and then furious.

'I would never do that!' she declared. 'It would be the very last thing in my mind.'

'You're quite sure?' he asked coolly. 'Women make outrageous statements when they're alarmed.'

'It's you who are outrageous!' she declared stormily. 'I can't think of anything less attractive than being in love with you. No feeling woman could possibly live with you!'

He laughed without humour.

'I've only known one feeling woman in my time,' he told her harshly, 'and she turned her back on me when I needed her most. Now I please myself how I live and I don't think Salty is coming to any harm. In your heart perhaps you don't believe that either,' he suggested.

'I still think she should have a proper education,' Andrina said lamely.

'You mean a conventional one, of course. That will come in good time,' he declared. 'I'll send her to school in Barbados when she's ready to go.'

'She'll be a rebel by then!'

He smiled at the suggestion.

'Aren't we all? Salty will make her way by herself. Trust her!'

She felt exasperated by the man, for no good reason except that Salty had touched her heart from the moment of their first meeting.

'I still think you're wrong,' she declared, stepping back

as the sun glinted into her eyes. 'I think you're taking the easy way out, but really it's no affair of mine.'

'As you say.' He stood above her, silhouetted against the glare of sunlight with the red stallion straining at the rein in his hand. 'The alternative doesn't appeal to you, I take it?'

She gazed back at him, unable to see the true expression in his eyes for the blinding rays of the sun, then she took another step backwards, stumbling on a protruding palm root.

Instantly his hands were on her arms, supporting and imprisoning her at the same time as, deliberately and callously, he bent his dark head to kiss her on the mouth.

'Think about it,' he said, 'if you have nothing better to do.'

The touch of his lips had turned her world upside down and for a moment the sun seemed to spin around them with a dazzling brightness which threatened to blind her. The singing of the surf and the rustling of the palms beat like a persistent pulse in her brain, dimming the past and obscuring the future. Then, suddenly, Ward had set her free and was leading the way up from the beach on to a narrow path which led along the cliff.

Drawing a swift, steadying breath, Andrina followed him, although all her strength seemed to have been sapped by that one curiously demanding kiss. Furious that her legs refused to carry her, she said harshly:

'Don't wait for me if you're in a hurry. I simply can't lose my way when there's only one path.'

He glanced back at her, smiling.

'I can wait,' he said.

She followed him up the incline beneath the trees until they reached a narrow bridle-path running parallel to the shore.

'Do you want to ride?' he asked. 'It's a fair walk to the hotel.'

'I walked on the way out,' she began.

'And now you're limping,' he pointed out. 'Did you

hurt your foot when you tripped just now?'

Almost deliberately he was reminding her of that kiss, of their nearness as he had held her back there on the shore, but she would not let him see how much it had affected her.

'It's nothing,' she declared. 'Walking back to Castaways will do it good.'

When they had reached the highest part of the road Ward turned to point down through a narrow ravine to the ocean far below.

'You can see the village from here,' he explained. 'It has a small harbour and a good stretch of sand.'

'Black sand,' she said, thinking that his side of the island reflected his character as nothing else could have done.

'Volcanic—yes, but I think our side of Flambeau is more dramatic. Certainly it's far more rugged than Tamarind.' His eagle gaze swept upwards to the twin peaks in the north. 'We share the mountain, of course, but it's never visited its wrath on Tamarind.

'Has it erupted recently?' she asked, immediately interested, although a faint chill of fear settled on her heart.

'Not for the past hundred years. Too long for anyone to remember, although the village has its legends.'

'Such as?'

'Oh, there's a resident demon, of course, who lives comfortably in the crater, growling only once in a while!'

'Have you heard him growl?'

'Frequently,' he said. 'It wasn't pleasant.'

'Yet it didn't chase you away?'

He laughed.

'What put that idea into your head? I couldn't have run even if I'd wanted to.'

'Because of the Caribs and the fishermen?'

'Something like that.'

Andrina looked up at him, aware of his height and the broad sweep of his shoulders and shaken by a desire to know him better.

'I suppose it would mean complete extinction if the lava did flow down to the village,' she said.

'It would change Flambeau out of all recognition and cost innumerable lives.'

She shivered involuntarily.

'It's difficult to accept among so much beauty,' she said.

'The demon waiting in the depths?' Ward turned to lead the stallion down the slope. 'Surely you've stumbled on him somewhere, even in faraway England?'

'There are all sorts of demons,' Andrina admitted. 'Loneliness and sadness and loss and even—disillusionment.'

He looked at her closely.

'Is that why you came to the Caribbean?' he asked.

Taken by surprise, she could only tell him the truth.

'It was part of my reason.'

'Disillusionment is something we feel when we're sorry for ourselves,' he said, 'or when we can't handle life. We have to learn to live without everything we want, otherwise it becomes impossible. Out here,' he added, looking across the acres of bananas he cultivated, 'compensation is easy to come by. There's a whole world of freedom on an island like Flambeau.'

Compensation for regret, she thought, and even disillusionment.

'It's easy enough to understand,' she agreed as Salty came riding towards them from the road over the Bluff. 'Will you allow her to come to Castaways occasionally?' she asked impulsively. 'Someone will see her safely back to Nettleton's.'

He frowned.

'I don't want her to become a nuisance.'

'She wouldn't be,' Andrina assured him as Salty drew the donkey to a halt. 'Please give it a trial.'

Ward smiled.

'You're very kind,' he said almost formally.

Before the child had reached the junction of the two paths he had mounted the stallion and galloped away, and

Andrina was left with the impression of the little donkey being fended off in case her friendship with Salty should become too intense.

'What did Prentice want?' Gerry asked when she went slowly down the path towards the hotel. 'I saw you coming along the bridle-path,' he added, taking in her scanty attire. 'Did he turn you off the beach? "No trespassing, by order!"'

'On the contrary,' said Andrina, wondering how long he had been watching their slow progress along the cliff, 'he was quite kind. He rescued my beach-bag for me while I was in the water because it could have been taken for an interesting piece of flotsam by one of the natives.'

'They're primitive enough to consider anything left on the beach as their natural property, given to them by the sea,' he agreed, the frown still creasing his brow. 'Are you encouraginig Prentice or the child?'

Andrina flushed.

'Neither, but Salty might come over to sail in the lagoon and I think we should make her welcome. She's a lonely child and she should be encouraged to mix with other children when we have them at Castaways.'

'Does Prentice share your view?'

'He didn't exactly object.'

Gerry glanced at her sideways.

'I wonder why?' he mused. 'It would be one way of getting a foot in the door.

She drew in a deep breath.

'I think he would ask outright for anything he wanted, He's that sort of person,' she decided.

'I don't trust him,' said Gerry. 'His main ambition is to own the whole island and your aunt is standing in his way. He wants to turn Flambeau into a vast estate—to turn back the clock, in fact, so that he can make all the rules.'

'He's already made quite a success of Nettleton's, from what I can gather,' Andrina pointed out, 'and Castaways could easily be part of it.'

'It's what he would like.' Gerry rattled his fingers along

the wire of the cockatoos' enclosure to make them screech. 'The man in authority with a finger in every pie!'

'He could hardly want Castaways as it is at the moment,' Andrina pointed out practically. 'Things have been allowed to slide a little, don't you think?'

'We manage all right,' he answered almost truculently. 'People appreciate this sort of thing.'

'Not when the drains don't work!' she pointed out. 'Gerry, you'll have to see reason. My aunt has been ill, but that's no excuse for allowing everything to fall apart. If I'm going to stay I mean to square things up.'

'A nice little new broom!' he teased. 'But you'll come to see it our way, in the end, Drina, when you get Ward Prentice out of your system.' He put a careless arm about her waist. 'You could be barking up the wrong tree, you know. People come here to "get away from it all", so let's face it, you could be tidying your aunt out of a good living by making Castaways just another island hotel.'

She wondered if he might be right, but she was determined to insist on a few improvements, although she had done that at Nettleton's to no avail.

Surprisingly, Ward came to Castaways two days later. Gerry had crossed to Grenada with the launch to pick up the incoming guests and her aunt had made her appearance on the sheltered side of the terrace for the first time since Doctor Harvey had sailed away.

'I feel fighting fit now,' she announced. 'Going to Barbados will be a great waste of time.'

She hadn't said that she wouldn't go, however. Andrina noticed the omission, realising that Belle must still be feeling weak, and suddenly she wondered about the advisibility of the awkward journey to Barbados. It would involve the uncomfortable crossing to Grenada, the bumpy taxi-ride to the island airport, and the subsequent flight on an Islands plane, and her aunt had said not so long ago that she was nervous about flying.

It was the only way, however, short of the specialist coming to Flambeau, and that was probably out of the question as there was no real emergency.

After lunch Belle dozed comfortably in the shade of the giant oleander at the end of the terrace while Andrina took the opportunity to go for a swim, choosing the north end of the lagoon rather than repeat her adventure on the white sands to the south. Wandering leisurely along the beach in her bare feet with one of her aunt's straw hats perched forward on her head to shield her from the direct rays of the sun, she saw Salty riding across the Bluff and coming down through the palms towards the hotel. When the child saw her she steered the donkey towards the beach.

'Hullo!' Andrina greeted her. 'Are you going to swim?'

Salty considered her for a moment in silence.

'I haven't brought a costume,' she said, digging her heels into the donkey's flank to urge him on to the hard sand near the water's edge. 'We were just riding out.' She got down from the saddle to tether her mount. 'This donkey's in a bad mood,' she volunteered. 'I'll have to tie him up.'

'I can lend you a costume,' Andrina offered. 'It's a bikini, so it shouldn't be all that big.'

Salty gave the idea her undivided attention.

'I often swim with nothing on,' she remarked tentatively.

'Try the bikini, all the same,' Andrina smiled, taking it from her yellow bag and holding it out for inspection.

'Why do you have two?' Salty wanted to know.

'In case I decide to sunbathe once I've been in the water.'

'It's pretty,' Salty admitted. 'I like blue.'

'It would match your eyes.' Suddenly Andrina was thinking of another pair of eyes, equally blue and equally penetrating. 'You're welcome to try it,' she added hurriedly.

Salty stripped off on the beach, dancing around on the warm sand when she had slipped into the lower half of the bikini. She was like a young faun with her cropped hair and large, luminous eyes which were now full of laughter.

'I'll race you!' she challenged, dashing into the green water. 'We'll swim to the jetty and back.'

It was a fairly long swim, but they rested in the cool water under the jetty, floating with their legs stretched out before them for several minutes until they were ready to return.

Andrina looked up the beach towards the hotel and was immediately aware of Ward Prentice watching them from the shadow of the trees. He had been standing on the terracing beside her aunt's chair, but he moved forward as they turned to swim away. She felt her heart hammering against her side. Why had he come? What did he want at Castaways when he had already acknowledged the fact that they were uneasy neighbours?

Increasing her stroke, she just managed to beat Salty by a hairsbreadth as they drew parallel with the yellow beach-bag.

'We must do this again,' she suggested as they waded out. 'Will you come back to the hotel for something to eat? An ice-cream, maybe?'

Salty's eyes widened.

'I'd like that,' she agreed. 'I never have ice-cream. It's bad for my teeth.'

'One won't make any difference, and you can always ask permission when we get to Castaways,' Andrina pointed out.

Salty nodded, peeling off the bikini to wring it out. 'It's very pretty,' she said again.

'Next time you can bring your own,' Andrina suggested.

'I've only got a pair of drawers—old ones,' Salty informed her. 'I wear them on *Sea Hawk* when we go to Grenada or St Lucia to pick up stores.'

'You like going there?'

Salty nodded, struggling into her faded jeans and pulling the blue T-shirt over her head. Her hair was treated to a brief shake which set her half-dried curls bouncing as she untied the donkey.

'Will he walk along the road?' Andrina asked.

'Sure!' Salty pulled the rein over the reluctant beast's head. 'C'mon!' she shouted into his left ear. 'Show willing!'

Concealing her amusement, Andrina followed the unlikely pair till they came to Castaways where Ward Prentice was waiting. He had moved away from the terrace edge and was sitting beside her aunt when they came in through the hallway and there was a cool drink at his elbow served, no doubt by Pete, who was hovering in the background. When Andrina halted in front of them he fixed her with a challenging smile.

'I'm taking your aunt to Bridgetown,' he said. 'The journey across by Grenada is too much for her.'

Without having to ask whose decision it had been, Andrina said:

'I'm sure we're both very grateful. Thank you very much.'

'I take it you won't come with us?' he asked.

Andrina hesitated.

'I think I ought to stay here and—manage things.'

He looked amused.

'I thought Fabian did that,' he said without renewing his invitation. 'I'll pick you up tomorrow,' he turned to say to Belle. 'Early, I'm afraid, if we're to get back in reasonable time.'

It was all so casual, just sailing away into the blue for a whole long, perfect day with a trade wind behind them and Ward's steady hand on the wheel. As soon as he had left Andrina knew that she had wanted to go very much.

Instead, she rose early the following morning to see them off. Ward had sailed *Sea Hawk* round the Bluff as the sun came up, anchoring in the Cove as her aunt was finishing her breakfast.

'You should be coming with us,' said Belle. 'You'd enjoy Bridgetown.'

'Will Ward bring you straight back?' Andrina asked.

'I'm not sure. He'll be going over on business and I'll have to wait his convenience. I thought the child might be going.'

'Salty?' said Andrina. 'Is he leaving her behind?'

'It would appear so,' Belle answered, looking towards the schooner now anchored in the lagoon. 'If she's aboard at all

she's generally perched cross-legged on the bowsprit or
running along the deck.'

There was no sight of Salty anywhere, not even in the
dinghy which Ward sent ashore for his passenger.

'I wonder what she'll do with herself all day,' Andrina
mused. 'It's a terribly lonely life for a child.'

'I wouldn't tell Ward that, if I were you,' said Belle,
stabbing a pin into her straw hat to anchor it for the
journey.

'I already have,' Andrina admitted. 'It didn't go down
very well.'

'I should say!' Belle laughed. 'His authority is seldom
questioned, especially by a woman.'

'You don't really like him?'

Belle considered the question, her brows drawn.

'I wouldn't say that exactly,' she decided. 'We're two
strong characters, I guess, both determined to have our own
way, both thinking we know what's best for Flambeau. We
ought to be able to live peaceably and Ward can be helpful
on occasion—like now, for instance—but Gerry thinks he's
only biding his time, waiting to pounce when the opportunity presents itself. It's a worrying thought, even though
I can see his point of view. Castaways isn't exactly worked
as it should be, but it suits my way of life, and all my
memories of Albert are here.'

She got into the tender, sitting majestically in the stern
and turning to look back at Castaways as Garson rowed
strongly towards *Sea Hawk* where Ward was waiting.

Andrina stood on the jetty, waving to her until she finally
boarded the schooner, thinking that she should never have
let her go alone. Of course, Ward was with her; of course,
she was safe enough when she knew Bridgetown so well,
but might she not have needed the understanding of someone of her own sex in this emergency which she had never
expected?

'You wanted to go,' commented Gerry when she made
her way back to the hotel. 'Why didn't you?'

'I suppose I felt I could be more useful here.'

'Keeping an eye on me?' he suggested.

'Gerry, you know that isn't true!' she protested. 'You've been at Castaways a long time and my aunt trusts you. It was just that I seem to have deserted her, turning her over to a stranger.' She began to tidy up the chairs which were scattered round the pool. 'What's Ward Prentice trying to do on Flambeau?' she asked suddenly.

'Buy up all the land,' Gerry said calmly. 'Then he can turn us out whenever it suits him.'

'It's—difficult to believe.'

'Don't let him fool you! It's what he wants.'

'Why?'

'For obvious reasons. With all the land in his possession, his ambitions would be fulfilled. It must have been how the original settlers felt when they first came to the Islands. It was absolute power.'

'And Salty?'

He shrugged.

'He's fond of her, of course. He was very much in love with her mother at one time, but she married his brother instead. After Salty was born he came back for a little while, but most of the time he prowled around on *Sea Hawk* living the sort of life he preferred.'

'What happened to his brother?' asked Andrina.

'Richard? Oh, he couldn't bear to live at Nettleton's after Nola died, I guess.'

'Is that why Ward took over? To save the estate and make a home for Richard's child?'

He turned over on the cane lounger to look at her.

'You give him all the credits,' he accused her. 'I don't suppose Salty came into it for one moment. It was Nettleton's he was after. Richard and he were partners of a sort; they owned the estate between them, only Richard had the largest share. Ward preferred the buccaneering life, but that all ended when Nola died. He came back and settled down, and I have to admit he's done wonders for Nettleton's. As for Salty,' he added, 'it was just something he had to do. He really hadn't much of an option.'

'Did his brother sell his share in the plantation to Ward?'
He shrugged.

'Nobody knows for certain. It's something we have to take for granted.'

Andrina stood looking down at him as if she still found difficulty in believing what he had just told her.

'I wouldn't worry about it too much,' he advised, getting lazily to his feet. 'It won't get you anywhere with Prentice.'

She turned away.

'I was curious,' she said briefly. 'That was all.'

He came to stand beside her on the edge of the pool.

'What are you going to do with yourself this afternoon?' he asked.

'Think up some new menus.'

'There's no future in keeping your nose to the grindstone all the time,' he pointed out. 'Work, if you must, this morning and I'll take you to the village after lunch.'

It was an enticing offer, although there seemed to be plenty for him to do around the hotel.

'I have to go for fish,' he added, as if he had read her thoughts.

'In that case we needn't feel guilty,' she smiled. 'I'd like to see the village, and my aunt said something about a Carib settlement——'

'We could go that way,' he agreed. 'There isn't a lot to see—a few huts and a trading shop where they sell woven baskets and straw mats, but it does give you some idea what can be done for these people. Sometimes I think it would be better to leave them entirely alone,' he mused. 'They're amazingly content.'

They drove out in the mini-moke, getting the benefit of the breeze from the Atlantic as soon as they climbed the ridge which effectively divided Flambeau in two. Behind them lay the scrub country surrounding Castaways and the lagoon, before them, sloping gently to the west and south, lay all the well-tended land which was Nettleton's, the spice and nutmeg groves, the vast sea of the banana plantations and the fields of sugar-cane swaying gently in the wind. Mahogany and cedar crowned the higher slopes, with ebony and satinwood in between, a vast panorama of good husbandry flourishing under the watchful eye of the mountain which stood guard in the north. Inlets and a river estuary scalloped the rugged coast far beneath them and a little way along the road they came to the first of the Carib settlements.

Gerry stopped the mini-moke, which was immediately surrounded by a group of silent children who gazed at them, wide-eyed, as they got out. The hut ahead of them was obviously the village shop and a dark-eyed girl appeared from nowhere to attend to them.

'You can safely pay them what they ask for their stuff,' Gerry advised. 'They haven't heard of the big profit margin yet.'

Andrina bought some beautifully-woven mats which she thought would be useful at Castaways and they smiled goodbye. The children proffered some wild grapefruit and a cocoa pod, which she also bought, remembering what Ward had said about them giving value for money. He didn't want them to beg.

Driving on, they plunged down suddenly to the native village which had grown up where the river entered the sea. There was a tiny harbour, not yet complete, and several fishing boats moored to a stone quay. The fishermen themselves were busy with their nets, tying them between the palms, but there didn't seem to be much sign of fish.

'We have a regular order,' Gerry explained, leading the way to a boarded-up building which looked completely deserted. As they approached, however, two native boys made their appearance, smiling happily at their arrival.

'Good catch today, Mr Fabian,' they announced. 'Very many fish in net. You take yo' pick.'

They glanced shyly at Andrina, who smiled back at them.

'This is Mrs Speitz's niece from England,' Gerry explained. 'She's come to stay at Castaways.'

The information obviously pleased them.

'We ver' glad you come, ma'am,' the taller of the two said. 'We like you see our village when Mr Prentice give us this gran' new harbour.' He waved his hand in the direction of the fishing boats. 'Before, it was much difficult to pull the boats across the beach an' now we have great protection from the storms.'

On a day like this it was difficult to imagine a tropical storm tearing in across the ocean to fling itself against the island in savage fury, but the wide Atlantic lay just beyond the new harbour wall and anything was possible.

Andrina stood looking down at the boats while Gerry purchased the fish. Presently one of the native boys followed him out of the boarded store with a wicker basket on his head which he placed in the mini-moke.

'You come back Tuesday?' he enquired.

'Possibly,' said Gerry. 'See you have good fish!'

It was all very easy-going and good-natured, this bartering for the produce of the sea, but Andrina got the impression that a fair bargain had been made, probably at Ward's insistence.

As they drove upwards again through the sugar-cane she thought that she recognised the road.

'We must be getting near Nettleton's,' she guessed.

'It's all Nettleton's,' said Gerry, looking about him. 'As far as the eye can see.'

After the sugar-cane there was a vast stretch of papaya and yams and sweet potatoes in cultivated strips on one side of the road; on the other the ragged banana fronds tossed in the wind. Gerry put his foot down on the accelerator, hurtling along the corniche-like road as if in a mad desire to reach the summit of the ridge in the shortest possible time, but suddenly he was forced to apply his brakes and steer into the side of the road.

'Damn that child!' he muttered as Salty came cantering towards them on her donkey. 'She pops up all over the place, and always on the wrong side of the road.'

'It's hardly a freeway,' Andrina observed, watching as

Salty slid from the donkey's back. 'Gerry, I don't think she's very well.'

Salty was swaying on her feet as she regarded them vaguely.

'I feel sick,' she said with a slight tremor in her voice. 'I want to throw up.'

Andrina was out of the mini-moke almost before it came to a standstill.

'You've been riding too long in the sun,' she said. 'You should have brought a hat.'

'It blows off,' said Salty. 'It's down there on the beach. It went into the sea——' The blue eyes were suddenly glazed.

'She's ill,' Andrina said over her shoulder. 'Gerry, we've got to get her out of the sun. We'll take her to Castaways where I can look after her.'

Gerry had taken in the situation at a glance.

'We're much nearer Nettleton's,' he pointed out. 'The house is only a stone's throw away. If we made the journey to Castaways over that rough road she *would* be sick.'

Salty clung to Andrina for support.

'I want to go home,' she whimpered, so unlike her old, buoyant self that Andrina grew genuinely alarmed. 'That ol' donkey threw me again——'

Andrina felt a stab of anger go through her. What was Ward thinking about to allow the child to ride out alone on an unreliable animal, especially when he was away from home?

'Is there anyone else at Nettleton's?' she asked. 'Someone to take care of you?'

Salty looked more sorry for herself than ever.

'Only Berthe, an' she's too strict.'

'That wasn't what I meant. We must get you to bed, out of the sun. Is there anyone who can nurse you?' Andrina asked.

'There's Carrie, but I don't like her too much. I guess it will have to be Berthe.'

Andrina looked quickly in Gerry's direction.

'Do you know them?' she asked.

'Berthe has been a kind of cook-general at Nettleton's for years,' he said. 'She lives there with her husband and numerous offspring who work on the estate. She's a grand character, really, the genuine old "mammy" figure of the plantations. Her children and grandchildren are legion!'

'But you think she's too old to have full responsibility for someone like Salty?'

'By far!' he agreed.

'And Carrie?'

'Oh, she's a flibbertigibbet, if ever there was one. Always after the boys!'

'Is there anyone else there?'

'Nobody that I know of. There was once a Miss Simmons who was a governess of sorts, but she went off to Grenada on some ploy or other and didn't return. Prentice advertised, I suppose, and Miss Simmons is what he got.'

So he didn't try again, Andrina thought.

'She was a retired schoolma'am with a chip on her shoulder,' Gerry remembered.

'Poor Salty,' said Andrina. 'No wonder she ran wild.' Her arm tightened about the little girl's shoulder. 'We'll soon have you inside, Salty,' she promised. 'It's the sun that's making you feel so bad after your fall.'

They came to Nettleton's with its semi-circular frontage and the rows of windows overlooking the ravine. Moving through the garden it was almost uncannily still, with no wind to disturb the palms and a bright sun beating down through their leaves. It made a shining halo round the topmost fronds, slanting down to the tropical growth at their feet like a flashing sword. The scent of spice was suddenly heavy on the air. Sharp and pungent, it seemed to fill the whole garden, cinnamon and ginger and nutmeg cancelling out the sweeter perfume of the flowers. The jade-vine had shed tender green blossoms on the strip of grass under the terrace wall and over the semi-circular steps leading to the main door.

On her former visit Ward had taken her on to the terrace

and in by one of the long windows, but now they entered by
the conventional way because the door lay wide open.

The stillness inside the house seemed even more oppressive than the silence in the garden, but Salty seemed to
accept it as normal.

'They'll all be asleep,' she said. 'Everybody goes to sleep
after lunch.'

While you're left to your own devices, Andrina thought.

'Anyone alive?' Gerry bellowed helpfully. 'Berthe, are
you there?'

The silence prevailed for a moment longer to be broken,
at last, by the sound of heavy footsteps moving across a
polished floor in a kind of inner hall which stretched along
the back of the house.

'I'm comin',' a warm, cheerful voice announced. 'I'm
comin' as fast as ever I can!'

Andrina turned to find herself face to face with Berthe
for the first time. She was a big, handsome Bajan woman
with a polished black face and kind black eyes which took
in the situation at a glance.

'Yo' be fallin' off that stupid donkey again, Miss Salty!'
she declared. 'He not safe, an' you know it. Mr Prentice,
he ought to buy yo' one proper pony an' be done with it.
That donkey, he know when he can take de upper hand all
right. He jus' bide his wicked time to throw yo' 'cause yo'
gettin' to be too heavy for his lazy back!' She nodded
brightly in Andrina's direction. 'Yo' from de hotel, I
dassay?' she guessed, still with an eye on Salty. 'What yo'
done with yo' head?' she demanded.

'I grazed it.' Salty's voice faded to a whisper. 'I feel sick,'
she repeated.

Andrina took the situation in hand.

'She must lie down,' she explained. 'If you could prepare her bed——'

The old woman was suddenly full of concern.

'Yo' think she proper sick?' she asked, moving towards a
broad flight of stairs which led to an upper floor. 'I take yo'
up right away.'

Salty leaned heavily against Andrina as they mounted the stairs.

'Don't leave me,' she begged plaintively. 'Don't go away.'

'I won't,' Andrina promised. 'An hour in bed out of the sun may be all you need.'

They climbed the staircase after the native woman, reaching a wide gallery that went round three sides of the hall.

'Here we are!' Berthe fussed, opening one of the solid old mahogany doors which led from it. 'I go make yo' something to drink,' she decided, leaving Andrina to cope with the medical side of the situation.

'I wish I knew what to do,' Andrina said to Gerry over her shoulder. 'She looks as if she might faint.'

Between them they lifted Salty on to the small four-poster bed which occupied one side of the room.

'I'll close the jalousies,' Gerry decided. 'Too much sun in the circumstances. If you ask me, she has a mild concussion from the fall and a touch of sunstroke into the bargain.'

Andrina's heart seemed to miss a beat.

'If only this hadn't happened when Ward was away!' she sighed.

'We can't order accidents to our own requirements,' he reminded her, stepping back from the window in the green light which came through the closed shutters. 'Are you going to stay with her?'

'What else can I do?' Andrina looked down at the thin brown fingers fastened so determinedly on her own. 'She needs someone to look after her.'

'There's Berthe,' he pointed out.

'I suppose so,' Andrina acknowledged, 'but I'll stay for a while, all the same. She may only need a rest.'

Gerry put the palm of his hand against the child's forehead.

'Golly, she *has* got a temperature!' he exclaimed.

It was something Andrina had suspected ever since they had set out for Nettleton's.

'I'll sit with her for a while,' she said. 'Do you want to

go back to Castaways with the fish?'

'If I don't it's going to smell to high heaven in all this heat,' he said. 'Tropical fish are never at their best for keeping, especially the flying variety. You must eat them straight out of the sea to preserve their flavour.'

'You can leave a few,' Andrine suggested. 'Perhaps Salty will eat something once she's slept for a while.' The fingers clutching hers were suddenly relaxed. 'I think she's asleep now.'

'I half expected her to keel over coming through the garden,' Gerry admitted. 'She's such a frail-looking scrap, just lying there.'

There was nothing of the almost aggressive, boyish little girl left as Salty lay back among her pillows, the thin cotton bedspread pulled up under her chin. The bed seemed to engulf her, dwarfing the spare little body completely as she flung one hand out to reach for comfort.

'Don't go!' Her lips barely formed the words. 'Promise. Promise faithfully!'

'I won't go, Salty,' said Andrina. 'I do promise you. I'll stay till you're well.'

Gerry crossed to the door.

'I'll make myself scarce,' he said. 'It seems as though you might be here all night.'

The thought pounced at her in the dim green twilight of the shuttered room.

'Come back for me,' she said, 'when you can.'

He went reluctantly, passing Berthe in the doorway as she returned with a jug containing some beverage of her own concocting.

'We'll leave her to sleep for a while,' Andrina decided, looking down at the shadowed face on the pillow. 'Her pulse is good, but she's still fevered.'

'She take on like this once, a long time ago, when she first come back fro' that New York,' Berthe said heavily. 'Poor scrap, she done miss her mother then an' Mr Ward, he no' understand. He too angry after all that happened. He ver' good man, but he angry when folks are bad. M's Prentice was bad. She no' care much about Mr Richard, an' he done love her ver' much. Mr Ward, he angry because he bring her to de island in de first place.'

Andrina knew that she was listening to nothing but crude gossip, yet it was impossible not to listen.

'M's Prentice, she no' like Flambeau ver' much. She like that ol' New York, an' after a while she done went off with Miss Salty an' everything. She don' want to stay here any mo'. She don't want anyone to love her after that, I guess.'

'There must have been a lot of love in the beginning,' Andrina heard herself say.

'Oh, der was, der was!' Berthe sighed. 'More love than yo' could count on yo' fingers in de beginning. She had all de things she wanted, all of Flambeau fo' her very own!'

'Why did she go?'

Berthe looked uncertain.

'I dunno! Maybe de ol' devil in de mountain frighten her.'

Andrina smiled faintly, feeling curiously uneasy in the presence of this sudden revelation. Ward and Richard's wife, she thought. Had Nola Prentice been Ward's before his brother had come on the scene and stolen her away and was that the reason why he had never married? Was he—could he possibly be still in love with a passionate memory, and was that why he had taken Salty into his personal care? Nola's child, the little girl who might have been his own!

It was all so much conjecture based on Berthe's disapproving words, but it was difficult to thrust aside sitting here in this shadowy room watching over a child she had only met a few days ago. But Salty had wound tentacles of love and pity around her sensitive heart and she knew that she would stay.

Till Ward came? Till he found her sitting there, where Nola should have been, without being asked?

Her heart thudded hard against her side as a man's heavy tread sounded on the stairs, but it was Gerry who came into the room and not Ward. He had brought her overnight bag.

'I found all you'll need in your room,' he explained, laying the bag at her feet. 'I thought you'd want to stay since there's no sign of Prentice coming back.'

'Would he bring *Sea Hawk* in at Tamarind?' she asked, trying to sound unconcerned. 'He wouldn't come round to the harbour?'

'Not if he had your aunt on board. He'd make the lagoon and then sail round the Bluff. Something must have delayed them in Bridgetown, for there's a fairly stiff wind blowing in from the Passage which would have made the return trip easy enough.'

'They'll be here in the morning, I expect, and I do hope Salty will be well by then,' said Andrina.

'Where will you sleep?' he asked, looking out through the open door.

'In here, on the sofa.' She was determined not to upset Ward's household any more than she could help. 'I'll borrow the quilt from Salty's bed.'

Gerry stood uncertainly in the middle of the polished floor.

'I ought to stay with you,' he said.

'There's no need. Really, Gerry, I'll be all right, and you'll be more use looking after Castaways.'

'It's a funny old world,' he mused whimsically as he turned to the door. 'I wouldn't mind if you'd thrown yourself at me.'

She flushed at the implication.

'I don't feel that I've "thrown myself" at anyone!'

'Prentice is bound to think so,' he said bluntly. 'The kind of women he's known in the past have all been willing victims. It's an epidemic of sorts out here, women offering their favours without being asked, and Prentice is the sort of man they generally go for.'

'He may be, but I've already told him I wouldn't "go for" him for all the tea in China!'

'You don't say?' He shot her an incredulous glance. 'Did he make a pass at you?'

Again she flushed, remembering Ward's strangely compelling kiss.

'Nothing so obvious,' she said. 'I think he was looking for a—new governess for Salty.'

'And you firmly declined the position?'

'Quite firmly. I hardly thought I qualified for—what he wanted.'

Gerry laughed abruptly.

'Perhaps you do now,' he said. 'He's bound to feel grateful after all you've done.'

'Salty came first,' she said truthfully. 'I couldn't have done anything else.'

He looked down at the flushed face on the pillow.

'Has she slept all the time?' he asked. 'Did you get her to eat anything?'

Andrina shook her head.

'I thought it best to leave it to nature. Children sleep things off fairly easily. She could be her old bouncing self in the morning.'

'I hope so. I'll come back for you then,' he promised.

She watched him go between the jalousies, standing with her hand against the window-frame as he started up the mini-moke and drove off down the road. Dear Gerry! He wasn't half so lazy or half as hard-boiled as he tried to make out.

Another hour passed while she dozed fitfully on the rather hard sofa at the foot of Salty's bed, and then Berthe came in with her supper on a tray.

'Yo' like it better downstairs?' she asked.

'No, Berthe, this will do fine,' Andrina decided, looking over at Salty. 'I'll try not to waken her.'

'She look much better now,' said Berthe, 'but don' yo' go away. She need yo'. An' yo' jus' holler if yo' want more food. I done mak' yo' coffee with rum in it to mak' yo' sleep!'

Andrina ate the appetising fish concoction she had prepared, finishing with the rum-laced coffee and two small coconut cakes which were delicious.

'I've really enjoyed that,' she said when Berthe returned for the tray. 'You're a good cook.'

The old woman grinned broadly, her fine white teeth flashing as she accepted the compliment which she took as her due.

'I learn to cook long time ago, in America,' she said proudly. 'Then I go marry that man Aaron, an' he bring me here to Flambeau. We been here long time,' she added. 'It ver' good place an' Mr Prentice ver' good boss.'

Andrina pushed the tray aside.

'And that was a very good supper! Don't let me sleep too soundly, Berthe, after all that rum,' she said.

'Rum be good medicine,' the old woman assured her. 'Yo' sleep well, missy. Ver' sound!'

Whether it was the effect of the rum or just the silence of Nettleton's, Andrina slept until dawn broke, waking with a start of guilt when she realised that it was light. Yet she knew that even a slight movement from the bed would have brought her wide awake at any time during the night.

Healing sleep had settled Salty more easily among her pillows and the high flush had gone from her cheeks. She still breathed heavily, but it seemed that the worst of the fever had gone with the hours of darkness.

Glancing at her watch, Andrina saw that it was five o'clock. There was no sound anywhere and she turned over to snatch another hour of sleep. Whether she dozed or had a nightmare she was not quite sure, but she imagined she heard a deep growling coming from somewhere beyond the garden. From the mountain, she thought, in swift alarm.

Struggling into a sitting position, she peered towards the door. Someone was standing there, looking at her, a tall, dark-visaged man in a long sea-cloak which he had thrown carelessly across his shoulders. He came towards her.

'What are you doing here?' Ward demanded. 'What's gone wrong?'

Andrina pulled the thin sheet up to her chin, angry because she could feel the high colour of embarrassment mounting to her cheeks as he watched her.

'I didn't come deliberately,' she said, 'and please speak

quietly in case you wake Salty. She has some sort of fever, but I think the climax is over. We found her on the road from the village, too near to Nettleton's not to bring her home.'

The final word seemed to disturb him, though he made no reference to it, standing in the doorway stern-faced, waiting for her to continue.

'It would have been foolish to take her to Castaways,' she finished lamely.

'Very foolish.' He moved towards the bed where he stood looking down on the small, sleeping figure with deep concern in his eyes. 'Perhaps, when you're dressed, I can take you back there.'

'I'd like to be sure about Salty,' she protested. 'She seems a great deal better for a good night's sleep, but she shouldn't be allowed to get up right away.'

He put a gentle hand on the child's brow as she stirred in her sleep.

'She's over the worst,' he said. 'Her temperature has dropped. I don't think you need worry about her any more.'

He turned away from the bed, standing with his back to her as he looked out of the window at the early light chasing the shadows from the garden, and suddenly he seemed to fill the whole room. She saw him as a man overwhelmed by circumstances yet still determined to mould his world in his own way, a man who had turned his back deliberately on the past to fasten his eyes steadily on a future of his own making.

When she had struggled out of her impromptu bed and wrapped her dressing-gown around her, she asked:

'Have you taken my aunt back to Castaways?'

He shook his head, turning to look at her as he passed the bed.

'It would be better if we talked downstairs,' he suggested. 'Get dressed and I'll send Berthe up to sit with Salty.'

He looked deliberately at the overnight bag Gerry had brought from the hotel and she knew that he resented her presence in the house, although he had once suggested it as a permanency. But why remember that distressing incident, she thought, or the demanding kiss which had followed it?

'I didn't come prepared to stay,' she said coldly. 'Gerry brought my bag over from Castaways when we realised that Salty was practically alone in the house.'

'She's often alone,' he said brusquely. 'It doesn't seem to do her any harm.'

Without waiting for her reply he closed the door behind him and walked away along the corridor towards the staircase.

Quickly Andrina got into her clothes. The dress she had worn to ride across the island in the mini-moke with Gerry was no longer fresh, but she washed in the miniature bathroom adjoining Salty's room and pulled it over her head with a new determination in her heart. Whatever Ward Prentice thought, she was doing this for Salty and not 'throwing herself at him' like all the other women he had known—with the possible exception of Salty's mother.

He was waiting for her in the downstairs hall. All the windows had been flung wide open and she knew that he had done this as soon as he had come in. Beyond them the garden lay still and quiet, while far below the palms slanted motionless across the black sand of L'Anse Deux Feux.

'What's happened to my aunt?' she asked, her concern obliterating the original embarrassment of their meeting. 'Is she here?'

Perhaps it had been more convenient for him to bring the schooner in at the harbour without chancing the entrance to the lagoon.

'I had to leave her behind in Bridgetown,' he said. 'But don't worry too much,' he added swiftly. 'There's nothing seriously wrong.'

Andrina sat down on the nearest chair.

'We didn't expect anything like this!'

'No,' he said. 'Your aunt wanted to come back, but it was a question of a second opinion. The man she saw wanted a colleague to back him up, I suppose, and there was a question of treatment, something that had to be done right away. She was—concerned about Castaways, of course, and you being here on your own.'

'I should never have let her go alone,' Andrina said regretfully. 'I should have gone with her. Where is she now?'

'She booked in at a hotel she knew.' He led the way into a room panelled in mahogany with a magnificent view across the ravine. 'You'll have breakfast before you go back?' he suggested. 'I'll take you across in the jeep.'

'Gerry has offered to come for me,' she said involuntarily. 'You've been kind enough, helping my aunt.'

Ward smiled sardonically.

'Being "kind" isn't one of my virtues,' he reflected, 'and Berthe will be cooking for me, anyway, but you're free to make your own decision. Fabian may be late getting over if he's depending on the Moke. Where did you go yesterday?'

He shot the question at her as if he had been pondering it for some time.

'Gerry thought I would like to see the harbour and he had some fish to collect for the hotel. It's a standing order, I gather, and it all looked very fresh and appetising.' Suddenly she realised how hungry she was. 'I will have something to eat,' she decided, 'if Berthe has already cooked it, and then Salty may be awake and I can see her before I go.'

Ward walked out on to the semi-circular terrace to look down to the ocean rolling in towards L'Anse Deux Feux.

'I'm not the sort of guardian you would have chosen for her,' he suggested, 'but you would be surprised at the affinity we have for one another. Salty enjoys this sort of life and I'll be sorry when it has to end.'

'You'll send her to school in Bridgetown?'

'Eventually.' Berthe came into the room and he turned towards her. 'Miss Collington will be here for breakfast,' he told her.

'I's got it all ready,' Berthe informed him, 'an' a tray set for Miss Salty, if she can bear to eat even a morsel. You see her, Mr Prentice, pretty soon?'

'Yes, I'll go up.' He prowled to the far end of the room where a massive sideboard took up most of the space along one wall. 'I'm going back to Barbados on Tuesday,' he said, turning to face Andrina. 'If Salty is well enough I'll take her over for a check-up. What about you?'

'I'd like to see my aunt,' said Andrina, 'but Gerry could easily take me over to Grenada——'

'It's quicker—and cheaper—by *Sea Hawk*,' he declared, 'and you needn't feel too deeply obliged. You could spend some of your valuable time in Bridgetown choosing Salty some suitable apparel. A skirt, for instance. I don't think she has one.'

Before she could answer him or even make up her mind to accept his offer he had gone and she was left alone in the big, unfamiliar room staring at a portrait. It was the picture of a woman in a blue cotton frock painted not so long ago, and it hung in the most prominent position in the room, facing the door. She had not noticed it when she had come in because Ward had been walking ahead of her, but now she was face-to-face with Salty's mother and the blue eyes that were so like her daughter's were fixing her with a challenging stare. There could be no doubt about their relationship and little doubt about the fact that Salty had inherited her spirited character from the woman whose portrait remained the most dominant thing in the room. It hung above her like a challenge, and she felt that Ward kept it there for a reason of his own.

It would be generous to suppose that he did not want Salty to forget her mother, that the portrait must remain as the evidence of past affection so that she might grow up with the memory clear in her mind, but it might also mean that he had never forgotten the girl in the blue cotton dress, that he was still attached to her by the bonds of love and the pain of irretrievable loss.

Turning away, she waited on the terrace till Ward rejoined her.

'What did you think of the harbour?' he asked.

'It's not quite finished, is it?' she said. 'You seem to be enlarging it.'

'Making it bigger and safer,' he agreed. 'When I first came to Flambeau the fishermen pulled their boats up on the beach between catches. It was time-consuming and dangerous, but they hadn't any money behind them and they'd been doing it for hundreds of years, anyway. When they have a safe harbour to return to they'll be able to do more with their boats and the fishing will improve. They land some of their catch on Grenada, but Flambeau is their home. At the present moment the banana boats stand off and we load the crop by barge, but once the harbour is finished the boats can come alongside. As far as I'm concerned, it will simplify life at Nettleton's when we can load direct.'

'It sounds as if you're doing a great deal for the island,' Andrina suggested, immediately interested.

'And myself,' he answered promptly. 'Flambeau is a challenge and I have to make Nettleton's pay. You give me too much credit if you think I'm being entirely magnanimous where the islanders are concerned. When I see what I want I make an effort to get it. Why not?'

'Of course.' She felt slightly disconcerted by the apparent ruthlessness of his confession. 'So long as you're being fair.'

He laughed outright at her summing-up.

'I try to be,' he said. 'As fair as I possibly can.'

Yet she felt that he could be ruthless, too, if the situation demanded it. He would take what he wanted for Nettleton's and if it improved the lot of the islanders into the bargain that was all to the good. He would be a reasonable employer who would expect a fair return for the money he spent.

As they stood there on the terrace waiting for Berthe to return with their breakfast she thought that she could understand how he felt about Nettleton's, at least. He had called it a challenge and she knew that he would meet it

with determination and a good deal of hard work, shirking
nothing.

Below them, in the garden, a voice took up the words of a
calypso.

> 'The bee he come, the bee he go;
> He spread the pollen high an' low.
> The more he come the more he make
> To give me honey for my cake.
> The bee! The bee! De honey bee,
> He is so ver' good to me!'

The singer came into view, half submerged under a wide
straw hat. Evidently on his way to work, he greeted the new
day with a song, and Ward acknowledged the respectful
salute he offered.

'The next stanza should amuse you,' he said dryly. 'It's
pure calypso.'

> 'The honey bee he strong and straight,
> He give me honey for my cake.
> He strong and straight, like Mr Ward,
> Who give us all he can afford.
> He promise to be good if he
> Has plenty labour—you and me!
> He promise he will see us right,
> An' do us good with all his might!'

'It's sheer bribery!' Ward laughed.

'Or appreciation,' Andrina suggested. 'They know you'll
keep your word. It's fairly obvious that your side of the
island is flourishing. Nettleton's must be a showpiece.'

'You haven't seen it all,' he said. 'The next time you have
guests willing to walk more than a hundred yards, go with
them to the spice groves. They're well worth a visit. The
scent of cloves will be a lingering memory for you long after
you've left the island.'

The words were dismissive, as if he knew that she would
not stay.

'That might be some time ahead,' she told him. 'I couldn't possibly leave Castaways to its fate while my aunt wanted to return.'

He looked beyond her, down towards the black sand of L'Anse Deux Feux.

'She'll probably make her decision, one way or another, when you go to Barbados,' he said.

Berthe appeared with a heavily-laden tray which she set down on the wooden table overlooking the ravine.

'Miss Salty, she still asleep,' she announced. 'She sleep sound, like a baby. That ol' devil fever, he run away fast,' she added, glancing up at the mountain where all the malignant spirits had their abode. 'Did you hear dat mountain growl last night?' she asked. 'He growl good an' strong, but now he jus' mutter like thunder goin' off to someplace else.'

Ward dismissed her fearful utterance with a wave of his hand.

'There are no devils, Berthe, save of our own making.' His dark brows were suddenly drawn. 'Surely you know that?'

'I knows it, Mr Ward,' the old woman told him, 'but I jus' can't believe it. I think, sometime, dat ol' mountain he prove us wrong!'

Ward was still frowning.

'See to Miss Salty,' he said dismissively, 'and tell George I want to see him in the spice sheds in half an hour.'

'You ride out there pretty soon?' Berthe asked. 'You no' sleep ver' much.'

'I manage, Berthe,' he said more kindly as he pulled out a chair at the table for his unexpected guest. 'You just tell George what I said.'

The old woman hobbled away, shaking her head as Andrina sat down at the table. It was an odd experience to be taking breakfast with someone like the master of Nettleton's. Ward's frown had disappeared, but he still seemed to be concentrating on his conversation with Berthe.

'Is there really any danger from the mountain?' she

asked, looking up at the sleeping giant. 'Immediate danger, I mean.'

'I don't think so. It "growls" occasionally and that puts the fear of death into the natives, but so far it has only been a rumble in its sleep, the warning, perhaps, not to take too much for granted. If it should errupt——' He uncovered a silver dish to peer inside. 'If it should erupt,' he repeated, 'it would probably blow on this side. You would be safe enough at Castaways.'

'But the damage to Nettleton's might be considerable,' she finished for him. 'It could mean the destruction of everything you've achieved.'

He helped her to a portion of scrambled eggs.

'Everything,' he admitted. 'It would be curtains as far as we were concerned.'

Andrina watched him as he piled eggs on to his own plate.

'I hope it will never happen,' she said. 'Are we—prepared?'

She had used the plural subconsciously and she saw him smile.

'I can't answer for Castaways,' he said dryly.

'If there's something I should do——'

He shook his head.

'We can't fight nature on such a grand scale. We can only prepare for the worst and expect the best. I made my emergency plans a long time ago, and Castaways naturally came into them.'

She looked up sharply, remembering what Gerry had said about the land around Tamarind Cove.

'Of course we ought to work together,' she said, 'if we're working against the forces of nature, and I would have to accept your decision because I know so little about the island, but it's really a matter of making arrangements with my aunt or—or Gerry.'

'Fabian would sit tight at Castaways out of sheer inertia,' Ward said brusquely. 'I wonder that your aunt has been able to put up with him for so long.'

She drew a deep breath.

'We'll have to be content to differ on that,' she said. 'I gather she's very fond of him because he came to the rescue when my uncle died. She had nobody else.'

'Except you,' he reminded her, passing his plate for another helping of scrambled eggs. 'Fabian is completely aware of the fact, I'm sure. He came to the island five or six years ago and then disappeared for a while. Nobody seems to have any idea where he went, but he came back when he heard of your uncle's death. I dare say Mrs Speitz needed him at the time.'

'She certainly needed someone to help with the hotel,' Andrina agreed. 'She isn't exactly the managing type. My uncle seemed to do most of that and she was content to go along with what he wanted. They were very much in love.'

He considered her statement while he poured their coffee.

'Occasionally it seems to last,' he mused. 'You've been in love, of course?'

The abruptness of the question caught her off guard.

'Why do you say "of course"?' she parried.

'Because it isn't difficult to guess that you've been hurt,' he answered. 'You're guarded about the past because you're afraid your emotions might betray you a second time, but you can take comfort from the fact that most of us have had the same experience.'

'You'd certainly be able to handle it better,' she decided, pulling her coffee cup towards her. 'I can't imagine you being hurt by love.'

He pushed his chair back from the table, rising with an abrupt movement which dismissed what might have been a moment of intimacy between them.

'You could be right,' he said. 'And now I'll go and say good-morning to Salty if she's awake. Finish your breakfast and you can go up to her before you leave.'

Sitting at the table where he had left her, Andrina tried to come to some sort of decision about him. Ruthless he might be, but he had also been kind, seeing Belle Speitz

safely settled in Barbados before he had returned and probably reassuring her into the bargain. He had resented her
own presence at Nettleton's, but he had also been grateful
that she had cared for Salty in an emergency, although
whether he thought it had been necessary for her to spend
the night in his home she would never be quite sure. He
had been an excellent host, but he had also criticised her in
no uncertain manner, and he had also said that emotion
was the last thing she should expect from him. He seemed
to be relentless in his desire for supreme power, yet in a
brief, unguarded moment he had shown himself vulnerable,
like everybody else. He had been scarred by an unhappy
love affair, but he had probably dealt with it ruthlessly,
making no evident concession to the bitter past.

Quite suddenly she knew that she had not looked back
for days, that Flambeau with its demanding new interests
had given her a different perspective and a bright, wide
horizon for the future.

The sound of the mini-moke chugging along the dust
road brought her back to reality and she was standing at the
top of the terrace steps when Gerry drew up.

'I'm late,' he admitted, 'but there were things to do at
Castaways. Where's Salty?'

'Still in bed.' He came quickly up the steps to stand beside her and she knew that he had seen the two places set at
the table just inside the window. 'Ward came back. He's
upstairs with Salty now.'

'The devil he is?' Gerry exclaimed. 'Why didn't he bring
Belle straight to Castaways?'

'Because she didn't come back with him. I think he
would have come straight to the hotel if I hadn't been here
when he arrived,' Andrina explained. 'Aunt Belle had to
stay in Bridgetown for a second opinion.'

His eyes sharpened.

'What happened? Is she seriously ill?'

'I don't think so. Ward said something about treatment
which might be necessary.' She moved towards him down
the steps. 'Gerry, I'll have to go to her as quickly as pos-

sible. I should never have let her go alone in the first place.'

'You weren't to know all this would happen.' Comfortingly he put his arm around her shoulder, drawing her close. 'Leave it to me,' he said. 'Leave everything to me!'

'You're very kind.' She drew back from his embrace. 'But I'm saying that I want to go to Barbados at once.'

'We'll do that,' he agreed, still holding her. 'We'll do that right away.'

'We can't both go,' Andrina pointed out. 'There are ten guests coming in tomorrow and someone has to be here to meet them. It has to be you, Gerry. I don't know anything about taking the launch over to Grenada.'

'Then how do you propose to go?' he demanded.

'With Ward. He intends to take Salty over on *Sea Hawk* and I can go with them.'

'I see,' he said, his hands tightening their grip on her arms. 'It's all settled—just like that? I wonder what Prentice had to say to Belle on the way over. He never misses a trick.'

'It would be difficult to trick Aunt Belle in so short a time, and why should he?' Andrina demanded. 'He was doing her a favour, as I see it, and now he's offering me a trip to Barbados on the same terms. Salty is going with us and he wants me to supervise her new wardrobe. She certainly needs one!'

Before he could answer Salty had thrust her head out of an upstairs window immediately above them, and Andrina could see Ward standing behind her, half hidden by a curtain.

'I'm better, but I have to stay in bed!' Salty yelled before Ward's constraining hand drew her back into the room.

'I must go and say goodbye,' said Andrina.

'I thought you'd already done that,' Gerry observed dryly as he set her free, at last. 'Don't be long!'

Ward was not in Salty's room when she reached it.

'I'm better,' Salty repeated almost aggressively, 'but Ward won't let me go out. He says it would be taking chances and I have to wait and see how I feel in the morning. Then,' she added, her pale little face alight with anticipation, we're all going to Barbados—you and me and Ward—on *Sea Hawk*!'

The pleasure in her voice was infectious, and Andrina bent to kiss her on the cheek.

'Hop into bed and do everything you're told for a whole day,' she advised. 'It shouldn't be so very difficult, and then we can sail off on the schooner and really enjoy ourselves!'

'I wish I could go to Castaways with you,' Salty pouted.

'Some other time.' Andrina tucked in the cotton coverlette before she turned to the door where Ward stood watching them.

'The complete domestic scene,' he observed. 'You do it very well.'

It was almost as if he had closed a door in her face and all the warmth of the sunlit terrace where they had sat with their coffee was shut out.

'I take it you're still coming to Bridgetown,' he said on their way down the stairs.

'Of course—unless you've changed your mind about taking me.'

He smiled.

'I don't alter my decisions as easily as that,' he said. 'I'll bring *Sea Hawk* round to the lagoon at six-thirty. Be ready!'

He went out by the main door, a tall, strangely compelling figure in riding-breeches and a silk shirt which he had substituted for his sailing gear of faded shorts and cotton vest, and Andrina remembered his instructions to Berthe about George meeting him at the spice sheds. He was ready to ride out there now, but he had not renewed his invitation to her to go there.

Slowly she made her way through the cool hall to the terrace where Gerry was waiting.

'Ready to go?' he asked, glancing behind her as if he expected to see Ward at her heels.

'Yes.' She glanced back into the shadow-filled hallway. 'It's a sad sort of house,' she said, 'in a way. It's big enough for a whole family, but there's only Salty and Ward and two servants to make it look lived-in.'

He said, going towards the mini-moke:

'If you have any ideas in that direction you'd better forget them. Prentice isn't the marrying kind. He can get his women without tying too firm a knot.'

Andrina got into the uncomfortable Moke.

'Did you know Salty's mother well?' she asked.

'Everybody knew Salty's mother,' he said. 'She was a sensation. Ward brought her to the island on *Sea Hawk*, but she spent a lot of her time at Castaways. She was the life and soul of every party we had, and Richard Prentice fell head over heels in love with her.'

'In spite of the fact that she was Ward's girl?'

'More or less. Anyway, when they married Ward sailed off on *Sea Hawk* and didn't return until after Salty was born.'

'I see.' A vivid picture of the girl in the blue cotton frock flashed before Andrina's eyes. 'I suppose he's still half in love with her even now.'

'Nobody would be able to tell that.' Gerry started the engine. 'Prentice keeps his secrets, but when she died he brought Salty back to the island and took over Nettleton's when Richard went away.'

'Where did Richard go?'

Gerry shrugged.

'Your guess is as good as mine. Seems that Nola left him to go back to New York. She was an actress of sorts—Nola Burke.'

'Why did she take Salty with her if she went off because she wanted a career? Surely she would have left her behind with her father.'

'Perhaps she couldn't do that. Richard and Nettleton's she might abandon without a great deal of heartache, but her child might have been something different.'

'What happened to her?' asked Andrina.

'There was a fire at their hotel. She threw Salty out of the window. It must have been a terrible shock to the child.

She wasn't very old—about three, I think—but old enough
to remember. Nola died before the firemen reached her.'

Andrina caught her breath.

'Poor Salty!' she said. 'Why was it Ward who brought
her back to Flambeau?'

'Richard had followed Nola to New York but hadn't
found her. He was told she'd gone to Hollywood and he set
out for California before he heard about the fire. After that
—well, I expect he just couldn't come back here. Probably
he sold out to Ward on condition that Salty was given a
home at Nettleton's. It's the sort of bargain that Prentice
would make.'

'He's very fond of Salty.' Andrina felt that she had to
defend Ward. 'He wouldn't make a bargain like that just
for his own satisfaction. He may still be in partnership with
his brother.'

'You're mighty interested,' Gerry suggested tersely.
'Why?'

'No reason.' Somewhere deep inside she knew that she
was lying. 'It's difficult to live on an island as small as
Flambeau without wondering about its inhabitants.'

'Wonder about me, then!' said Gerry, leaning over to
plant a surreptitious kiss on her cheek. 'I'm well worth a
second thought!'

'You're impossible!' she laughed. 'Do you want to land
us in the ditch?'

CHAPTER FOUR

LOOKING around at Castaways Andrina decided that there was much to be done. The hotel had been run in an easygoing manner for far too long, and although she did not want to change the 'atmosphere' there were a few changes that could be made to its general advantage, and she set about making them.

Gerry looked on with a gleam of faint amusement in his eyes.

'You're a right little new broom,' he said, 'but you'll never change Castaways no matter how hard you try.'

'I don't want to change it,' Andrina protested. 'Just tidy it up. The parrots, for instance. They definitely smell!'

'That's Pete's job,' he laughed. 'We mustn't take it away from him or he'll be heartbroken or go jump in the lagoon!'

'Then be sensible and see that he does it properly. After that, we'll take a look at the bedrooms.'

'Not my province,' Gerry protested languidly.

She turned to face him.

'What exactly *is* your province, Gerry?'

He had to think for a moment.

'General factotum, I guess,' he decided. 'Manager, if you want to flatter me.'

'I try not to do that.'

'Oh, well, I do what I can in a general way, ferrying guests backwards and forwards to Grenada and keeping an eye on things. Sometimes I help with the accounts, but I have to admit I'm not too good at that. Your aunt does them, after a fashion.'

'I'm quite able to take over till she gets back,' Andrina said, 'but I'll leave you to handle the outside staff. Could we clear up all that jungle growth between here and the road? It looks untidy.'

'You certainly *are* a new broom,' Gerry laughed, 'but a very pretty one! Luella will go over the bedrooms with you and if there's any broken furniture Josh will see to it. He's a wizard with a saw.'

'You could start with the beach,' Andrina suggested. 'All those missing slats on the recliners could easily be mended, and it's a job that would keep you in the sun!'

When she had finally checked the bedrooms with Luella she thought about the chalets. The little thatched huts were ranged in a rough semi-circle round the stretch of grass which passed for a lawn, elevated above the beach on a rocky platform which gave them a panoramic view of the lagoon and Tamarind Cove, and each hut was furnished for a self-catering holiday with a tiny kitchen, a shower-room, one bedroom and a verandah lounge. All the little dwellings were smothered in vines, making colourful patches against the green of the jungle behind them, and it was this growth that Andrina had asked Gerry to cut away. She felt that it could be a potential fire danger if a forgetful guest had trouble with an oil-burning stove or someone threw a careless match.

The view of the beach and the Cove fascinated her and for a long while she stood looking down through the trees towards the lagoon, imagining a schooner anchored there and wondering about their neighbour at Nettleton's. It was a dangerous thing to do if Ward Prentice was the sort of man Gerry said he was, yet she could not help remembering how kind he had been to Salty. Kind but firm, she thought, bringing her up to acknowledge discipline although at first she had seemed like a tearaway.

She sighed as Gerry came towards her.

'All finished?' he asked. 'I've seen to the beach loungers, so now you can sit down in comfort. I checked the white ones round the pool as well,' he offered with a slow grin, 'so I've not been idle.'

'You deserve a drink,' she said. 'You look quite warm.'

'I'm going to swim,' he said. 'Coming?'

They swam in the lagoon, far out towards the reef, and he dived to bring her up small pieces of coral, pink and white and apricot-coloured, which she had admired from the glass-bottomed boat.

'It's much better with the snorkels,' he said. 'We can take them this afternoon. You'll love it, seeing all the fish darting about. It's magic!'

Andrina thought that he could turn most things to magic, succumbing to his infectious smile and his lighthearted approach to life.

'I'll race you to the shore,' he said when they heard Luella clang the bell to announce that lunch was ready. 'We've got Castaways all to ourselves at the moment.'

Walking up the beach with the sand warm under her feet, Andrina thought she had never been so happy nor felt so relaxed. In the shade of the palms she stopped to look at her companion.

'I'm going to kiss you,' Gerry said. 'You look like a dryad standing there dripping water all over the sand!'

'Surely you mean a sea-nymph,' she laughed. 'Dryads are generally found in a wood!'

'Does it matter?' He caught her round the waist. 'Drina, I really am in love with you,' he declared. 'We could make it together.'

She avoided his kiss.

'We've only known each other a couple of minutes,' she protested. 'You really can't be serious!'

'You think not?' He pulled her down on the dry sand under the palms, imprisoning her with both hands on her shoulders as he looked down at her. 'Try me!'

'Gerry,' she gasped, 'we're going to be late for lunch!'

Deliberately he kissed her, his fair head blotting out the sky and the waving palm fronds high above them.

'Give it a trial,' he begged. 'It's absolutely natural, and nobody would be more pleased than your aunt.'

Andrine broke away from him, running up the beach in an odd sort of panic as he pursued her to the terrace and finally dragged her, laughing, into the swimming-pool.

'Just to cool off!' he said, splashing fresh water into her face.

Wondering how sincere he was, she climbed out on the far side to reach for the towelling jacket she had left on one of the chairs.

'After lunch,' she said, 'I'd like to go to the spice groves.'

'As you decree,' he agreed. 'We'll take the Moke. It's far too hot to walk all that way in the sun.'

They ate at a table overlooking the pool in easy reach of the bar where Pete dispensed cooling Piña Coladas for them to drink. Luella herself brought a huge wooden bowl of salad and a platter of succulent chicken for them to eat, sitting down on one of the bar stools to watch them enjoy it while the little yellow birds who made the restaurant their rendezvous flitted to and fro between the garden trees and the wooden beams beneath the thatch. It was an idyllic situation which shut out time as the exotic blooms of jasmine and frangipani filled the air with their heady scent.

Lazily Andrina stretched in the sun, sipping her drink and thinking about nothing in particular except that it was little wonder that her aunt had decided to stay on at Castaways. No wonder she had been content there all these years—with her love!

'She must have been devastated when Albert died,' she said almost to herself.

'She was,' Gerry agreed, passing her coffee cup. 'She had nobody to turn to—except me.'

It was the reason why Belle was so fond of him, Andrina supposed. A deep gratitude for kindness at a time of bereavement was hard to cast aside, and in many ways her aunt and Gerry were fundamentally alike. They were both easygoing, happy personalities who had found their own particular Eden and were utterly content to live in it from day to day without a great deal of thought for the future.

'Do we need special permission to go to the spice groves?' she asked, her train of thought taking her to Ward Prentice whose outlook on life was so utterly different.

'Not really, though it's Nettleton country,' Gerry said.

'It's always been recognised as a showplace for our guests, something of special interest to boost the economy!'

He brought the mini-moke to the door while Andrina changed from her bathing-suit into a cotton dress.

'It's the colour of butter,' he said, looking her over with appraising eyes. 'Take a hat.'

She found her handbag and the finely-woven straw hat her aunt had given her, tying a yellow chiffon scarf round the crown to match her dress. There was a sense of excitement in the air, an anticipation of adventure to come, of something new in the offing which she was going to enjoy.

'Want to drive?' Gerry asked as they approached the Moke. 'I guess you ought to try if you're going to stay here. We use it all the time.'

'It looks positively dangerous!' she laughed. 'How old is it?'

'Only a couple of years. It could do with a bit of maintenance, I suppose, but it fills the bill. There's no point in driving over these roads in an expensive limousine.'

She got in behind the wheel.

'You're taking your life in your hands,' she told him as he climbed up to sit beside her.

Slowly they moved off, bumping along the rough track which led to Castaways while Gerry explained about the gears.

'You'll soon get the hang of it,' he encouraged her. 'There's a knack about getting into reverse, but I'll show you that later on.'

'Thank goodness there isn't much traffic,' she said. 'Do we turn left or right at the top?'

'Left,' he said. 'We go right along the spine of the island.'

They drove for nearly an hour at no great speed, the dust from the narrow road blowing up behind them like a thin grey veil, and then, suddenly, they were going down on the other side of the ridge and the scent of spice was everywhere. It seemed to quiver in the air, filling their nostrils with its aromatic fragrance, cinnamon and ginger and mace floating up through the trees to cast its heady spell on everything around them. There was a great silence when they stopped the mini-moke.

'We'll have to walk from here,' Gerry explained. 'It isn't far.'

They left their disreputable conveyance at the side of the road, walking down into the shade of the grove where the nutmeg trees grew thick on either side.

'They came from India originally,' Gerry told her. 'There's something repellent about the smell of spice.'

Andrina paused to draw a deep breath.

'I hadn't thought of it like that,' she said. 'It's strong— very strong and astringent.' Why was she thinking suddenly of Ward? 'I wouldn't call it repellent.'

'Overpowering, then,' he allowed. 'In certain winds the ships pick it up far off shore and the fishermen have been known to use it as a sure guide on their way home. Do you want to go down to the drying sheds or just wander about in the groves?'

'Both,' she decided eagerly. 'Ward said there was a lot to see.'

He frowned.

'Everything is most efficient,' he admitted, 'and I suppose it pays him very well. Certainly he doesn't have to scrape a living.' He turned down one of the narrow rides between the trees where the nutmegs hung in clusters with the filigree mace holding them securely to the branches. 'It's the soil that does the trick,' he added. 'Anything will grow on the sides of a volcanic mountain with the minimum of effort.'

'But it all needs a certain amount of co-ordination,' she pointed out. 'It doesn't just happen.'

'Point taken!' he grinned. 'But you have to be a demon for work to set it all up in the first place. Richard Prentice was like that at one time before he lost heart and gave it all up. In the end, his brother was extremely lucky.'

The scent of spice intensified as they walked deeper and deeper into the grove until it became almost overpowering, and then they were suddenly in full sunlight again, in a community of sheds surrounding a square which had been laid out to accommodate the harvest of the groves.

A toothless old hag in a tattered grey skirt and red blouse approached them, leaning heavily on a carved ebony stick.

'You like me show you nutmegs?' she enquired hopefully. 'I show you ver' good.'

Gerry waved her assistance aside.

'She's begging, and Prentice doesn't approve. He could give her work if she'd only tidy herself up and stop smoking.'

'She looks ill,' Andrina protested.

'Not a bit of it!' he declared. 'She's just bone idle. Old Hilda's never done an honest day's work in her life. Furthermore, she dabbles in magic—the ancient art of hoodoo. Some of the islands are still riddled with it, I'm sorry to say. Even now she could be casting a wicked spell on us!'

The old woman was scowling as she searched in the pocket of her voluminous skirt and finally she drew out a long-stemmed pipe which she proceeded to fill with a concoction of dried leaves. The blackened bowl was almost burned through, but she cradled it between her hands as if it was a great treasure.

'You go away,' she predicted, her penetrating black eyes fastened on Andrina. 'You go away an' you come back different. You find love an' lose it pretty soon.'

She had turned her back on Gerry, almost as if she had forgotten him, but when he told her to move on she challenged him with dark, malevolent eyes.

'You no' big shot,' she said. 'You no' Mr Prentice. This am all his land. Yo' jus' little man work for one woman over at Castaways. You never have big plantation like this.' She swept a black arm in a wide arc to include the spice groves and the distant banana fields which bordered Nettleton's. 'Yo' jus' go everywhere in noisy Moke an' block up roads like crazy, an' Mr Prentice, he angry. Ver' angry!' she muttered as she hobbled away.

'Whew!' grinned Gerry. 'I hope that wasn't a prophecy!'

He took Andrina by the arm as they entered the first shed where half a dozen women were squatting on the wooden floor separating nutmegs from the vivid red mace to place them in piles on thin sheets of canvas before they were graded and sent to the drying sheds. A strong smell of cinnamon pervaded the far end of the shed where the fragrant leaves were being stripped from their branches before being dried and rolled into the familiar shape seen in the shops hundreds of miles away from the island of their origin.

It was all so very fascinating that an hour slid by before Andrina realised how long they had been there.

'We ought to go,' she said, 'but perhaps we could come back some other time.'

'You haven't seen the drying lofts and the great bins of nutmegs ready to be weighed and packed. There's a consignment just going out.' Gerry pointed to a row of carts lining the far side of the square. 'Prentice must be shipping them this afternoon and that's why you were dismissed so summarily after breakfast, I dare say.'

By the time they had looked in at the drying process and watched the graded nutmegs being packed into sacks with Nettleton's blazoned in black across them, they had been in the sheds for over an hour and it was a relief to get out into the fresh air away from the cloying scent of spice, but they had yet to make their way back through the grove where the heady perfume seemed to press down on them as they walked uphill in the afternoon heat.

Before they reached the parked mini-moke Andrina was aware of confusion. Voices were raised in argument just ahead of them, high-pitched and querulous, with no one voice predominating, which suggested a certain amount of chaos at the top of the grove. When they came on the scene it was evident that Gerry's carelessly-parked conveyance was the cause of most of the alarm. A line of laden vehicles stretched back along the grove road for several hundred yards and ahead of it the leader was in obvious trouble.

Trying to pass the mini-moke on the narrow road, the cart had slipped sideways into the irrigation ditch and was hopelessly bogged down in the soft earth.

'Damn!' muttered Gerry. 'How did that happen?'

Andrina drew in a deep breath.

'You took more than your fair share of the road.'

'I guess so.' He forged ahead. 'I'll have to help straighten this out.'

They were still standing looking at the cart when Ward came on the scene, taking in the situation at one impatient glance. Sitting astride the big red stallion, he gave his instructions to the field workers in swift, clipped sentences which in no way concealed his anger.

'The trader has been in for over half an hour,' he informed them. 'Time, you may remember, is money, and she must be loaded before nightfall to get away on the morning tide. Get two planks of wood to put under the rear wheels and I'll see to the mules.'

He did not ask Gerry to help and it was quite obvious where he placed the blame for this unexpected delay. Andrina stood helplessly aside as Gerry got in to move the mini-moke out of the way. Ward's terribly angry, she thought, and no wonder! She saw him speak to Gerry, but he did not turn to look in her direction.

'Heave! Heave away!' After their fashion the field workers were enjoying themselves, smiling widely as the sweat poured down their faces and raising a great cheer when the wheels went free. 'She done move!' they shouted. 'She done move real quick!'

Ward stood aside as the cart trundled out of the ditch. He had dismounted to help with the rescue operations and his light riding-breeches and silk shirt were thick with ochre dust. Andrina went towards him.

'I'm sorry this happened,' she said. 'We should have parked the Moke elsewhere, but I suppose Gerry didn't think there would be so much traffic on the road.'

He fixed her with a penetrating stare.

'That's his trouble,' he said. 'Not thinking too deeply.'

'Will it make a difference? Not getting to the harbour on time?'

'No, we're all right now.' He glanced at his watch. 'With a bit of overtime we should make the tide.' His blue eyes narrowed as Gerry came towards them. 'Have you checked on the water situation on your side of the ridge?' he asked abruptly. 'We're getting low.'

'I haven't checked, but it's still running out the taps,' said Gerry. 'Nothing to worry about, would you say?'

'I would say you ought to check—regularly in this weather,' Ward told him. 'Your spring was low last time I saw it. Fresh water is essential to us at Nettleton's to wash the bananas, so we can't bail you out if your own supply runs dry.'

'There's no reason why it should,' Gerry declared. 'It's been there for several hundred years. We need fresh water for the pool and the guests' bathrooms and, of course, the kitchens, but that's all.'

'It's considerable if you think about the state of the spring,' Ward reminded him dryly, 'and I've absolutely no intention of diverting water from the Nettleton supply to accommodate holidaymakers when a crop is at stake. The bananas are Nettleton's life's blood and they have to be washed before they can be packed for shipping. If you think carefully, I'm not being too unreasonable, and if you need help to clear your spring I'll let you have all the men you'll need once the nutmegs are away.'

Gerry looked as if he might refuse the offer of help, but Andrina said gratefully:

'Thank you very much. We'll look at the spring and let you know.' She hesitated. 'I suppose you still mean to go to Barbados in the morning?'

'Certainly.' He looked at her impersonally. 'You haven't changed your mind, I hope? Salty is looking forward to the trip.'

Not only Salty, but me, Andrina thought, watching as he remounted the red stallion and rode away.

Gerry re-started the mini-moke.

'I'll drive,' he decided. 'We're running out of time.'

'And water!' She was determined to challenge him about the spring, to see what could be done. 'If Ward's right and we are getting low could we find another source?'

'Only what belongs to Nettleton's. Most of the natural springs are on this side of the ridge and, as he told you, he uses a lot of water on the estate.'

'I wouldn't have thought they *washed* bananas before packing them,' she mused.

'It's the only way to spot flaws and clean off the grime. It's essential, I suppose, and the shipping company won't accept them unless they're perfect. The flawed hands are discarded before they're boxed and the natives get them for free.'

'Do we use them at Castaways?'

'Occasionally. One flaw and the hand is cast aside. The rest of the fruit can be perfect.'

They drove on, wondering what to do about the water supply.

'Can we take a look at our spring on the way down?' Andrina asked. 'It must be fairly low if Ward noticed it.'

They found the spring on the side of the mountain, bubbling into a cavern of rock which served as a natural canopy to shield it from the sun.

'It's lower than usual,' Gerry admitted, 'but it could be blocked further down, of course. Hang on a minute and I'll go and see!'

He went off down the rock-strewn slope, disappearing eventually in the dense growth of scrub which ate up the path he had chosen, while Andrina sat in the Moke allowing the stillness of Flambeau to wrap her round. There were no trees this far up to encourage the little yellow birds which darted in and out of the restaurant at Castaways, perching on the beams beneath the thatch, and the silence could almost be felt, but out of the corner of her eye she was suddenly aware of a flash of colour, the vivid blue of a T-shirt as someone slid between the rocks above her. It could only be Salty, she decided, but what was the child doing up here on her own?

'Salty!' she called, but only an echo replied.

Half exasperated, she got to her feet. Could the child be playing tricks on her, a mischievous game of hide-and-seek to lure her among the rocks?

She looked round for Gerry, but he was nowhere to be seen.

'Salty!' she called again. 'I know you're there. I can see you among the rocks.'

Dragging the reluctant donkey by the rein, Salty made her appearance from behind a mass of scrub.

'I was coming,' she said before she noticed the mini-moke. 'I thought you were alone.'

'I am—at the moment. Gerry has gone down to look at the water supply. The spring is very low.'

'We've got plenty of water,' said Salty, coming to stand beside her.

'It isn't quite the same thing,' Andrina explained. 'The two springs are entirely separate. You need all your own water at Nettleton's for the crops.'

Salty nodded.

'Would you go away if there wasn't any water?' she asked, her brows drawn.

'Of course not! The spring will fill up again. It's just a temporary shortage. Maybe we have a blockage somewhere farther down,' Andrina suggested. 'Gerry's gone to see what he can do.'

Salty moved restlessly across the stones.

'I thought you could come to see my secret place,' she said. 'If you were alone.'

'We could go some other time.' Andrina could see Gerry's white shirt between the trees. 'Any time, Salty.'

'After we come back from Barbados,' Salty whispered. 'No one else has to know.'

'Of course not!'

The child came a little nearer.

'You'd have to promise,' she said. 'Not to tell where it is.'

'I promise,' Andrina smiled. 'Honestly and faithfully!'

Salty looked up towards the rocks.

'It's in there,' she said. 'A sort of cave. My father took me once, before he went away.'

The fact that she had been on the mountain with Richard surprised Andrina, but Salty must have remembered every detail of that long ago excursion when she had been able to find the cave again to make it her own special place.

A child's fancy, a secret whim? But Salty expected her to take it seriously and Andrina wondered if it was wise to encourage her. If Ward knew he would disapprove, she thought, but already she had committed herself to the child who had been driven out of sheer loneliness to dream up a fantasy world in a remote cave in the mountains. She saw Salty as both deprived and abandoned, although she had everything she could wish for in a material sense. Richard, she thought, had a lot to answer for, even though he had been devastated by his wife's tragic death and could no longer live on Flambeau.

It was Ward's part in it all, however, which puzzled her most. Why had he taken on the responsibility of both Salty and Nettleton's at a time when he had been free to rove the Seven Seas in *Sea Hawk* as he willed? Was it his overwhelming love for Nola which kept him on the island, the desire to care for Nola's child although the mother had obviously changed her mind about him and married his brother? Could he be living a tormented life, remembering her?

Unhappily she turned to Gerry as he climbed steadily up the slope towards them.

'Any luck?' she asked as he saluted Salty and twigged the donkey's ear.

'Not much. There was a lot of debris down there, but the main fault is in the spring.' He looked worried. 'There's really nothing we can do about it at the moment.'

Salty took his hand.

'You could ask Ward for some water,' she suggested.

'We've already done that,' he said, 'and the answer is "no".' He helped her on to the donkey. 'Not to worry, though. We'll win through.'

Salty dug her heels into the donkey's grey flank.

'See you!' she said laconically in a tone far too sophisticated for her years.

'She's an odd kid,' Gerry reflected, putting the engine into gear. 'A mixture of mother and father, I would say.'

'Did you know them well?' asked Andrina.

He shrugged.

'Well enough in the beginning, till Richard stopped his wife coming to Castaways.'

'Stopped her?' Andrina queried. 'Isn't that a bit old-fashioned in this day and age?'

'Not with someone like Richard. She had to be the Lady of Nettleton's and she disappointed him. Full stop!'

'But he still remained in love with her?'

'I guess so.'

She felt she couldn't ask any more questions. To probe any deeper might be to involve Ward Prentice, and that was something she didn't want to do.

When he steered the schooner into the lagoon the following morning she was on the jetty, waiting.

Gerry looked up from the well of the launch where he was tuning the engine for his departure for Grenada to pick up their incoming guests.

'All shipshape and Bristol fashion!' he said without smiling. 'The one thing I envy Prentice is that ship.'

'If we worked hard enough perhaps we could have a schooner of our own one day,' Andrina suggested without much hope.

'They cost a mint. The most I could hope for is a new launch,' he decided.

'It's all within the bounds of possibility,' she said, looking sympathetically at his efforts with the recalcitrant engine. 'Do you think you'll make Grenada?' she added doubtfully.

'Have to!' he said cheerfully. 'Otherwise we'll have very few guests and practically no whisky!'

A launch put out from the schooner and she saw that it was Ward's deck-hand who was steering it. Ward himself had elected to stay on board, and she could see Salty perched on the bowsprit waving with her one free hand to welcome her aboard.

'At least Salty is glad I'm going,' she said as Gerry helped her into the tender.

'She's got you firmly wound round her little finger,' he grinned. 'Take care!' he added. 'And bring Belle back with you.'

It meant something to him to think of her aunt safely returned to Castaways, and there was genuine warmth in her heart as she looked at him.

'I hope I can do that, Gerry,' she said. 'I hope we'll all be together again.'

He let go the mooring rope which Garson had cast to him and the launch took up speed, and before they reached the schooner she saw Ward standing at the gunwale, waiting.

Garson helped her to climb the accommodation ladder, but it was Ward's hand that guided her safely on to the deck.

'Three cheers!' shouted Salty. 'We're going to sail away!'

Andrina looked up to meet Ward's eyes, pale, baffling eyes in the early morning light.

'Salty gets over-excited occasionally,' he said. 'Last night I wasn't quite sure whether to let her come or not.'

'Because of the fever?'

'Partly, and partly because she disobeyed orders and went out on that ridiculous donkey. She's been told not to ride too far into the mountains.'

'She was quite safe,' Andrina assured him. 'We met her, but I had no idea she shouldn't have been there.'

It was evident that Ward was practising the discipline she had accused him of failing to observe, but she could not help wondering if he was going to be too hard on Salty in the end.

'She's very capable for her age,' she said, certainly not wanting to confuse the issue by mentioning the cave. 'I think she'll get by.'

The heavy anchor chain rattled on to the deck as the winch took it up and soon they were out beyond the reef, sailing before a fair wind with the sun on their faces and a new lightness in Andrina's heart. Somehow she knew that the voyage they were beginning was going to be memorable.

Salty came rushing along the deck, her fair curls dancing in the wind.

'Come and see where I sit,' she insisted. 'Right up there in front of the mast!'

They walked for'ard, hand in hand, while Ward helped Garson with the sails. As soon as the engines were shut off they were in a new world, a world of vast silence attuned to the gentle trade wind which blew them swiftly along. The experience was entirely new to Andrina and she revelled in it, closing her eyes against the sun as its comforting warmth caressed her skin.

'It's best if you take off your shoes,' Salty informed her. 'Then you can feel how warm the deck is. You can tuck them in behind the mast so as not to lose them,' she added helpfully. 'Ward gets cross when anything goes overboard.'

Andrina could not imagine anyone being in a bad mood on such a day. The sun was shining, the sea was blue, and they had a fair wind to speed them on their way among the tiny islands of the Grenadines. Ronde lay somewhere behind them, south of Flambeau, and Carriacou and Union and Cannouan took shape on the horizon as they watched. Soon they would pass Mustique and Bequia on their starboard bow as they drove eastwards to their destination.

Ward came to sit on the deck beside them, his feet bare and his hair ruffled by the wind. There was a look of vast contentment about him as he said:

'It's a day in a million, with just enough wind.'

'You love this life,' Andrina said involuntarily. 'If you had your way it's how you'd live all the time.'

He paused to consider her suggestion.

'I'm lucky,' he said. 'I can have it both ways.'

'You mean building a kingdom on Flambeau and sailing off when the spirit moves you?'

He considered her for a moment.

'More or less.' He filled a short, black pipe with tobacco, cramming it down into the bowl with strong fingers as he gazed ahead to the shadowy island they were approaching. 'On the other hand, I could be making sure of two strings to my bow if Flambeau were to fail or prove a disappointment. I could always go back to trading among the Islands. *Sea Hawk* is my lifeline as well as being absolutely necessary to life at Nettleton's.'

He stretched his long legs out on the sun-blanched deck, breathing deeply and so obviously content with the present moment that Andrina had to smile. He was a different being out here on the open sea with no responsibility to cloud his vision but the guiding of his ship to the harbour of his immediate choice.

'Out there,' he said, pointing to the west, 'is Mustique, and further north you can see Bequia. The peak in the distance is Soufrière on St Lucia. It flares up now and then, but so far it hasn't been too serious. It had a big blow-out two years ago, but there wasn't much damage then, either. The Lesser Antilles are all more or less volcanic throw-up, the mountain tops of a lost continent which finally gave us the Caribbean Sea.'

Andrina leaned back against the mast where Salty had tucked her deck shoes for safety.

'Every day becomes more enchanting,' she confessed. 'I feel I could stay here for the rest of my life quite happily. It really is an earthly paradise.'

It was a full minute before Ward replied.

'You've heard, of course, that nothing is ever perfect. Not for long, anyway. You'll see the Caribbean in a less generous mood if you stay at Castaways. There are storms here as violent as anywhere else, over in a few hours, perhaps, but still disastrous. We take them in our stride, I suppose, because we know they won't last. Inevitably the sun shines and we forget.'

'Our mountain is a volcano,' Salty announced with a certain amount of pride. 'All the devils up there eat fire.'

Her voice had quivered a little on the final word and Ward looked up at her, frowning.

'There are no devils on the mountain, Salty,' he said almost gently. 'You mustn't be afraid of them.'

Salty pursed her lips.

'Only the fire devils,' she murmured. 'They're truly bad.'

He did not answer that, preparing to steer the conversation in another direction.

'Suppose you show Andrina how to make Island chocolate,' he suggested. 'The sort of cocoa she drinks in England isn't quite the same.'

'I'm prepared to believe that,' Andrina smiled, following Salty along the deck while he rose to help with the sails.

In the galley they made the hot chocolate drink to Salty's satisfaction, dissolving a dark slab of chocolate in hot water and stirring in brown sugar from the Islands refineries to sweeten it to their taste. Ward kept a great sack of it on the galley floor, ready to hand for every occasion, and the little granules seemed to trap all the sunlight from the upper deck as they spooned it carefully into the mugs.

'One for Garson,' Salty demanded. 'You can take up one for Ward. Maybe he'd like a biscuit,' she added, one eye hopefully on the large tin lying on the sideboard as they went through the saloon. 'It wouldn't spoil my lunch, would it?'

'Not too much,' Andrina agreed, 'though you ought to ask.'

'Do you have to ask for *everything* you want?' Salty queried, following her up the short companionway with two mugs clasped firmly in her hands.

'Generally.' Andrina had put her mugs on a tray. 'You can come back down for the biscuits if they're allowed.'

'I'm very fond of biscuits,' Salty informed her, 'but we don't have them too often. Only when we have visitors aboard.'

'Perhaps today will be an exception.'

'What does "exception" mean?'

'A different sort of day—not quite like all the others. Singled out as unusual,' Andrina explained.

'Better?'

'Not always, but—yes, it could be better.'

'Do you want today to be special?' Salty halted at the top of the companionway to search for Garson. 'Something nice?'

'I feel it's going to be very nice.'

Ward came along the deck to take the tray.

'Biscuits?' he suggested.

Salty put her mugs down on the coach roof.

'I'll get them,' she offered. 'I know where they are.'

She disappeared back down the companionway and Ward laughed.

'Funny how helpful they are when it's something they want for themselves,' he observed dryly.

'Maybe we're all a bit like that,' said Andrina. 'What's a biscuit or two among friends!'

She saw his eyebrows go up and the odd smile that sometimes played around his mouth when he presented her with a challenge.

'You should know the answer to that,' he said lightly. 'Do we drink our chocolate here or take it aft where there is more shelter?'

Garson had put up canvas wind-shields with *Sea Hawk* in bold black lettering on either side of the well, providing a sun-trap for them to sit in when they ate their midday meal and Ward led the way back there with an ever-watchful eye on the sails. Garson was at the tiller and Salty staggered towards him with a mug in one hand and the box of biscuits tucked firmly under her arm. Ward retrieved her gaily-patterned mug from the coach roof, setting it down on the tray.

'She's Garson's willing slave,' he commented, 'and vice versa. He'd do anything for her and she for him. In a good many ways he tends to spoil her and sometimes she makes demands on him that are almost impossible to fulfil, but I suppose that's a woman's stock in trade.'

'You've got a poor opinion of us,' Andrina commented. 'Do you really believe we demand allegiance all the time and give nothing in return?'

It was the wrong question. She saw that instantly as his dark brows drew together and tried to relieve the situation with humour.

'You needn't answer that, since it would only be a man's opinion, after all!' she laughed. 'A woman's stock-in-trade is so vast that it can hardly be measured by any ordinary yardstick, and even *Sea Hawk* couldn't carry it all away!'

'I heard Salty asking you just now what "exceptional" meant,' he said, the frown receding as he sat down beside her. 'Do you think you gave her a true meaning?'

'To the best of my ability,' she smiled. 'I'm not a schoolma'am!'

'In no way, in the accepted sense,' he agreed.

'What does that mean?'

'You're not too dictatorial.'

'Drink your chocolate!' she commanded as Salty joined them, offering the tin of biscuits for their inspection.

'Perhaps, when you've chosen,' she suggested brightly, 'Garson could have another one.'

'No more!' decreed Ward, hiding a smile. 'It will spoil his lunch.'

'Is Andrina going to cook for us?' Salty asked, settling down with the mug of chocolate between her knees.

'I'd love to!' Andrina offered. 'It would be—sort of working my passage.'

'And keeping you independent?' Ward supplied.

'I wasn't thinking about it quite in that way, but it would be—repaying you a little for your kindness.'

'Don't embarrass me,' he said, standing up to relieve her of her empty mug. 'After all, my "kindness" is merely leading up to the fact that I need your help. I was quite serious when I said Salty needed more clothes. The ones she has are practically threadbare, and I do recognise that they grow out of things. We might also buy her a dictionary,' he added on a lighter note, 'and some books.'

By high noon Andrina had spent an hour in the attractive little galley preparing a meal under Salty's instruction.

'Ward likes things with lots of spice in them,' she declared, 'and sometimes he has a curry. It's very hot,' she added with a gesture of distaste as she dug crab out of a tin for the seafood cocktail. 'It makes my mouth all fiery.' The last word seemed to distress her, but in the next breath she was more concerned with her present task. 'Can I pour the sauce on now?' she asked eagerly. 'I like this pink one best.'

Andrine had discovered the shrimp sauce in a jar among Ward's store of tins and wondered if he would like it, although she suspected he would consider it 'the woman's touch' which he seemed to scorn.

He ate his generous helping without comment, however, sitting in the shelter of the canvas screen with his long legs thrust out half-way across the well as if he was content to enjoy himself for an hour or two before they reached their destination. Salty, seated beside him, began to nod.

'Shall I put her to bed for a while?' Andrina asked, immediately aware that the idea had amused him.

'Salty doesn't need to be put to bed,' he said. 'She usually sleeps rough where she drops, but if you must——'

'She'd be much more comfortable in her cabin,' Andrina pointed out, 'and she wouldn't wake up with a crick in her neck.'

'Salty!' he yelled. 'Time to sleep. Andrina will tell you a bedtime story.'

When she had laid a rug over the child's thin little body Andrina went back on deck. All the used plates had been washed and tidied away—by Garson, no doubt—and Ward was at the wheel.

'Come up and help to steer,' he called. 'You ought to feel the wind in your hair!'

She went aft, pulling the cotton band from her forehead to let her hair blow free. The wind had freshened, filling the sails so that *Sea Hawk* seemed to bound forward with a shout of glee, strong and powerful in her natural element which was the sea.

For a long while Andrina stood beside the wheel without speaking, watching as the waves sped by with a swish of triumph to merge themselves in the widening wake while the flying-fish darted above them, their silver wings glistening in the brilliant rays of the sun. It was sheer magic speeding along like this under the billowing sails, and another kind of magic tugged irresistibly at her heart. If only Ward could always be like this, the gracious host, the understanding guardian of a susceptible small child, the man in authority who could also be kind. She thrust her first harsh impression of him behind her to prolong the moment and then he said abruptly:

'How long will you stay in Barbados if your aunt isn't able to come back with you?'

She turned anxiously towards him.

'What do you suspect?' she asked.

His eyes changed colour, their vivid blue deepening to slate.

'Just that she's an old lady very much in need of a rest.' He turned squarely towards her, his hands fastening hard on the wheel. 'She may need specialised treatment which will keep her in Bridgetown for some time, but if she has to stay there she'll worry about Castaways.'

'It means a great deal to her,' Andrina acknowledged, 'but I don't know how she's going to look after it if she has to stay in Bridgetown for any length of time. I'd help, of course, but she hasn't taken me fully into her confidence about the hotel.'

He looked at her sharply.

'Surely you know she's left it to you?'

Her surprise was overwhelming and for a moment she could only gaze at him incredulously.

'We've never discussed—anything like that,' she said. 'Never—and I don't see how you can know.'

'I offered to buy it from her.'

'Oh——!' It was what Gerry had hinted at—his over-

mastering desire to own everything on Flambeau! 'You
won't win,' she said in a crushed sort of voice. 'I'll resist
you wherever I can!'

'And Salty?' he asked, ignoring her vehemence. 'Does
your disapproval extend to the whole family?'

'Salty is different,' Andrina declared. 'We've come to
trust one another.'

'Which means that you can't trust me?'

'You told me yourself you could make better use of
Castaways,' she reminded him.

'I could make better use of the land,' he corrected her.

'It's not for sale either.' Her lips closed in a determined
line. 'My aunt has said "no" and I'm repeating it. Nothing
you can offer, nothing you can do will make us change our
minds.'

The constriction in her throat almost choked her as she
stood beside him with the warm wind blowing against her
cheek and the image of her perfect day receding farther and
farther away.

'In that case, I must bow to the inevitable,' he said
evenly, 'but don't blame me for trying. I hate to see good
land going to waste, and that's exactly what's happening
between Nettleton's and Castaways.'

She knew how right he was, but could not tell him so.
Something harsh and obstructive had clamped down on
her heart, taking away the magic of their day.

When at last *Sea Hawk* sailed across Carlisle Bay with
the mountains of Barbados reflecting the last of the sunlight ahead of them she was almost glad that their voyage
had ended.

CHAPTER FIVE

WARD steered straight for the yacht club where he moored alongside a luxury yacht which took Salty's breath away.

'Ain't it big!' she said, imitating Garson who was also admiring the other craft. 'But I bet it can't sail half so good as *Sea Hawk*.'

'How's that for loyalty—and bad grammar?' Ward asked, looking down into Andrina's eyes as if they had never had a difference of opinion about anything. 'Loyalty is something well worth fostering in a child.'

'To make her your obedient slave?'

He laughed at the suggestion.

'I'd be trying to usurp Garson's place in her life and I've a strong feeling that you might come second if the chips were down. Are you still willing to guide her round the shops?'

'Why not? I'm still very grateful to you, and we'll be here all day tomorrow, won't we?'

He nodded.

'I think the best plan would be to take you straight out to St Thomas to see your aunt,' he said, 'then if she can't find you a room in her hotel you could come back to *Sea Hawk*. I can fix you up with a suitable berth and Salty would be delighted.'

The sun had almost disappeared as they drove along Highway One in the car he had hired outside the museum to take them to St Thomas and a warm, soft light lay on the rooftops of Bridgetown and out over the Deep Water Harbour where the giant cruise ships came in. Already the shadows of night hovered on the eastern side of the hills, lending a mystery which could almost be felt as they stood guard above the valleys, and all the way along the road they were overtaken by the workers of Bridgetown hurrying to their scattered homesteads on one side of the island or the other. Soon it would be dark and the velvet sky would be alight with stars; soon the raucous sound of changing gears would be overtaken by the sound of music as the happy Bajans flocked to the numerous bays and coves around the coast to sing and play the night away.

They reached their destination as Ward swung the car off the highway into a sand-covered side road which was no more than a track and drew up at the entrance of one of the smaller hotels.

In some respects it was rather like Castaways, hidden behind a thick growth of hibiscus, philodendrons and ferns, with cascades of bougainvillea dripping from the roof and hiliconium and oleanders crowding the side walks which led across a well-watered lawn to a group of chalet-type dwellings bordering the ocean. Here the resemblance ended, however, because Watersedge was immaculate. The thick vegetation which screened it from the road had been cut back and trimmed into a neat hedge full of blossom, and the terrace which led round the swimming-pool to the open-sided restaurant was swept clean of leaves. The shrubs in the surrounding borders had all been kept in check and were in full, magnificent bloom, adding their fragrance to the warm air which swept in from the sea.

Ward made his enquiries at the bar and they were directed to a luxurious flat in the grounds with a wide patio in front of it and vines screening it effectively from its neighbours on either side. Above it, on a cool balcony which formed the roof of the patio, a fair-haired young woman was sprawled on a cane lounger.

'You looking for Mrs Speitz?' she asked in an incisive American voice. 'She was here a minute ago.'

'Thank you,' said Ward. 'We'll wait.'

Through the wide glass window which led on to the patio Andrina could see a large room with a table and chairs and a comfortable-looking sofa piled with cushions. Colourful Bajan rugs adorned the walls and a huge lamp full of sea-shells with a long conical shade stood on a satinwood table near the door which opened on to a narrow hall.

Salty skipped gleefully round the house, reappearing to announce that there was nobody there, and Ward pulled forward a lounger for Andrina.

'Would you like to sit down or would you rather go to the beach?' he asked.

They could hear the soft pounding of surf beyond the row of coconut palms which screened the apartments from the shore, but darkness was falling rapidly and the beach was likely to be deserted.

'I think we'd better wait here.' Andrina searched the shadows that lay across the lawn. 'She can't have gone far.'

'She likes this place,' said Ward. 'Possibly because it reminds her of Castaways in some respects. It also gives her a certain amount of privacy which she wouldn't find in a large hotel.'

Certainly he seemed to understand how her aunt would feel if she were undergoing a course of treatment and needed to rest.

'Will she cook for herself?' she asked. 'She really ought to be looked after.'

'All her meals can be served from the restaurant,' he explained. 'She can put in an appearance there or not, as the spirit moves her. There's a kitchen behind the main sitting-room in the apartments and a good-sized bedroom with a bathroom attached, so you have nothing to worry about. Your aunt will be well cared for at Watersedge.'

Before Andrina had time to settle in her chair Belle Speitz came hurrying along the flagged pathway from the entrance lobby, looking so bright and relaxed that some of Andrina's fears were quickly allayed.

'My dear, I can't tell you how sorry I am at not being here when you arrived,' she declared, kissing Andrina on both cheeks. 'I had a session at the hospital at three o'clock and they insisted that I relax afterwards with a cup of tea. You have no idea how kind they are!'

'I'm glad,' said Andrina, waiting for Ward to greet her aunt. 'Perhaps I can take you back to Castaways when I go.'

Belle looked doubtful.

'It will be a week or two,' she said. 'It's the sort of thing that shouldn't be done in a hurry, they say, and I sure can't dictate to them when they've made me feel so special.' She looked across the patio in Ward's direction. 'Thank you for bringing Drina across,' she said. 'It was kind of you to offer.'

'I was coming anyway,' said Ward. 'Salty is due for a check-up to make sure she isn't harbouring some bug or other, so we'll be invading the hospital tomorrow if you have to go back there.'

'I'm due every other day,' Belle told him, offering Salty a chocolate from the large box she had brought from the sitting-room. 'They're all soft centres, strawberry creams and fudge and peppermint. You'll love them.'

Salty gazed at the enormous box wide-eyed before she turned to Ward.

'Can I?' she asked. 'They're very bad for me.'

'One won't do you any harm,' he decided indulgently.

Salty took a long time to consider her choice.

'I think that one will be cherry,' she said, 'and I like fudge, but this one is really *big*, isn't it?' She selected a large candy wrapped in gold foil. 'It looks very good.'

'Don't let the outer wrappings fool you,' Ward cautioned. 'It could be quite different inside!'

'Are you here for a short stay?' Belle asked, leading the way into the living-room. 'I would have thought you wouldn't want to leave Nettleton's at this time of year.'

'I have a good foreman,' said Ward, 'and the work on the harbour is almost finished.'

'Nettleton's runs on oiled wheels,' Belle said without rancour. 'Sometimes I envy you.'

'We're hardly in the same line of business,' Ward pointed out, settling his long body into one of the deep recliners.

'You're so efficient,' Belle mused. 'I've often tried to be, but it didn't work. Perhaps I decided long ago just to drift.'

He looked at her keenly.

'How do you feel about coming back?' he asked. 'When

your cure is complete, I mean.'

Belle met his gaze with a faint smile in her eyes.

'Castaways is my home,' she said simply. 'I couldn't live anywhere else. Not now.'

They spoke about the voyage across and where Andrina could stay while she remained on Barbados.

'She can have a berth on *Sea Hawk*,' Salty announced eagerly.

Belle Speitz looked from the child to her niece.

'I can see you two are in a plot to plunder Broad Street,' she laughed. 'Are your plans already made?'

'Only vaguely,' Andrina began.

'Andrina has promised to supervise Salty's wardrobe for me,' Ward said briskly, 'but that won't take more than half a day. I'll be returning to Flambeau on Thursday, so it looks as if we have a deadline.'

'Maybe it would be better if Andrina stayed on the schooner, in that case,' Belle decided. 'We're very full here and the management don't approve of us sharing apartments. You'll dine with me, of course. I'll be happy to have you,' she added warmly.

Salty's blue eyes interrogated Ward's, but for a moment he hesitated.

'You'll have a busy day tomorrow,' he reminded her.

'Once in a while,' said Belle with her slow smile, 'rules should be broken. I won't keep you late, I promise.'

Gradually the initial reserve with which she had met her neighbour was thawing into a mood of acceptance and the atmosphere was almost friendly by the time they sat down to their meal in the restaurant at a table overlooking the sea. The sound of the surf pounding on the unseen beach before it ran in over the sand was the true voice of the Islands, and out across the bay a full moon hovered above the horizon like a giant lantern waiting to throw the long shadows of the coconut palms across the lawn.

The food was excellent and Salty enjoyed herself immensely, choosing from a long menu which she studied carefully, pretending to read.

'Paw-paw!' she exclaimed with satisfaction, recognising some of the letters she had learned. 'With *cream*!'

Andrina wondered if Ward had taught her her alphabet. She was a highly intelligent child and would pick up new ideas wherever she found them. Perhaps he had taken the time to instruct her, after all.

As the moon took over, banishing the darkness and most of the stars, a steel band began to play in the adjacent hotel. The muted sound, coming in across the silence of the garden, seemed to underline the magic of the night, and presently they were aware of a small procession approaching across the sand. Men bearing torches walked barefooted beside the sea, leading a group of dancers who obviously toured from one hotel to another willing to demonstrate the art of limbo dancing and the fascination of calypso. Salty stood up to watch, her face tense with excitement.

'Will they come in here?' she asked. 'Do you think they'll stop and sing?'

'No doubt!' Belle laughed. 'They come to entertain the hotel guests.'

The group of Bajan minstrels circled the tables, serenading the diners in turn, quick-witted when it came to calypso and the need to improvise.

'Little lady with the curly hair,' they sang to Salty,
'Who could resist your innocent stare?
Your blue, blue eyes and your tilted chin,
Every heart you are sure to win!'

'They know I'm not a boy!' Salty gloated. 'Imagine that!'

The musicians made a wide circle under the trees, playing softly in the moonlight for the guests to dance, and several couples took the floor. The lingering spell cast by these exotic, enigmatic islands held Andrina in its grip once more as the rhythm of limbo and calypso sobbed across the silence and Ward asked her to dance.

Surprised by this unexpected show of gallantry, she allowed him to lead her on to the wooden platform which

served as a floor, feeling the strength of his taut brown body
as his arm went about her waist and he took her hand in
his. His nearness, which had disconcerted her in the past,
seemed natural now as they moved together under the trees.
He danced well, circling the floor with an ease and assurance which was part of him although it vaguely surprised
her. Where and when had he learned to dance so well?

Questions were irrelevant, she decided, giving herself up
to the sensuous pleasure of moving in his arms to the
rhythmic beat of drums and the strumming of guitars. The
moments you stole from the pattern of life were sometimes
the most precious of all, she thought. Without speaking,
they seemed to be moving in a world of their own which
was far removed from Flambeau and the conflict of argument. Removed, perhaps, from reality, although for the
moment it did not seem to matter very much.

They were on the far side of the improvised dance floor
when the music ceased and Ward did not lead her back to
the table immediately. Instead, he drew her out to the edge
of the clearing where they could look at the sea. A shimmering pathway of gold led down from the moon across the
water almost to their feet, and by its light his profile was
strong and clear. He did not look like a man with a griev-
ance or one who would turn circumstances to his own advantage whenever he got the chance, yet she could not
dissociate that strong jaw from her first vision of him as the
pirate aboard his marauding ship waiting to take what he
wanted from life without question because of his own un-
doubted strength.

'What are you thinking about?' he demanded.

'You.' It was useless to lie to him while those piercing
blue eyes searched hers, expecting the truth. 'You're quite
different tonight—utterly amenable.'

He laughed outright.

'Because I let Salty stay up late?' he asked. 'I honestly
don't think it will do her any harm since she slept most of
the afternoon.'

'I wasn't thinking about Salty,' she said.

'Then——?' He put the question quizzically, his tone amused.

'It occurred to me that you might relax more often—to your own advantage.'

'That's true,' he agreed, 'although it might be difficult at Nettleton's. What would you suggest?'

'I don't know enough about your way of life to pass an opinion,' she answered honestly, 'but it does seem as if you think of nothing but work. It looks as if you've set yourself some kind of—goal which makes it impossible for you to relax.'

He allowed her comment to sink into the silence for a moment.

'You could be right about the goal,' he said, 'but I really don't feel the need to relax. When I'm working on Flambeau I have all I need.'

The coldness which had crept into his voice sent a quick chill to her heart.

'Which means that you're completely self-sufficient.'

'I try to be.' He hesitated. 'Andrina, my goal is to make Nettleton's pay its way so that Salty can always be assured of a settled background, of not having to want for anything that money can buy. She was deprived of love and affection at a very early age and it's up to me to see that she has something to put in its place.'

'All you can give her, all the money in the world and the comfort it can bring, won't make up for love.'

'I know that. Perhaps when I asked you to come to Nettleton's as my wife I was nearer a solution than I realised, but as you turned me down the matter must remain closed.'

'You know you weren't serious,' she said with a small quiver in her voice. 'You were trying to disconcert me because I had sounded pompous!'

He did not contradict her as the dancers took the floor again and the rhythm of limbo throbbed in the night air. Two men with long poles stepped forward, placing a third one across them as a dancer in skin-tight scarlet trousers and a silk bandeau took the floor, his dark body gleaming in the light of the torches like polished ebony as he gyrated to the music, bending over backwards to glide on his bare feet, slowly and assuredly, beneath the horizontal pole. It was an accomplishment so full of skill that it took Andrina's breath away. Lower and lower went the pole and still the smiling performer slid beneath it without his hands or body touching the floor.

'It's impossible!' she whispered. 'He just can't go any lower!'

As if to refute her argument, two of the supporting dancers came forward with raised torches to light a flare in the centre of the pole and the swift, decisive movement seemed to galvanise Ward into action. Firmly he took her by the elbow, leading her quickly round the cleared space to the table they had occupied during their meal. It was empty.

'My aunt must have taken Salty back to her apartment.' Andrina looked up to see Ward's face distorted in the light of the flares. 'What's wrong? What do you think has happened?' she asked.

'I hadn't thought about the limbo dancers,' he said tersely. 'Nola died in a fire and Salty was there.'

'Aunt Belle will know what to do.' Andrina ran by his side. 'Don't worry!'

He nodded.

'I'm sure she can cope, but I think Salty will feel better when I get to her. I've tried to shield her from this sort of experience until she can forget.'

'It won't take long. She's still very young.'

'And vulnerable.' His eyes searched the darkness. 'I should have remembered about the dancers.'

Belle Speitz' apartment was ablaze with light when they reached it and Belle herself was standing at the patio door. She put a cautioning finger against her lips as Salty appeared behind her, rushing to the shelter of Ward's arms. He held her close to him before he spoke in a level, matter-of-fact tone.

'Were you and Mrs Speitz trying to get away from us? You see now that it can't be done!'

Salty turned to Andrina with a forced smile.

'You won't go away?' she begged. 'You'll come back to *Sea Hawk* to sleep?'

Andrina glanced at her aunt.

'It would be most convenient,' said Belle, 'and save me asking favours. Probably you would be more comfortable on *Sea Hawk* and you could go straight to the hospital in the morning. The afternoon would do for shopping and you could have dinner with me in the evening again. I'm afraid there won't be any more limbo to entertain you,' she added as she saw the uncertainty in Salty's eyes. 'The dancers only come here once a week.'

Salty brightened perceptibly as she clung to Andrina's hand.

'Please come,' she repeated. 'You can have my cabin, if you like.'

'We'll manage without moving you,' said Ward, ruffling her hair. 'Say goodbye to Mrs Speitz and don't forget to thank her.'

Salty turned to Belle, throwing both arms about her neck.

'Thank you,' she said. 'I'm sorry I cried.'

'We all do on occasion.' Belle embraced her warmly. 'For different reasons, of course, but I guess it helps now and then. I'll see you tomorrow, Salty, and—take good care of Andrina when you go to Bridgetown.'

'We may go to the Animal Flower cave if there's time,' she announced. 'It's a long way, but we could take a taxi.'

Andrina turned to Ward.

'She has the whole day planned in advance,' he said. 'I've never seen her so enthusiastic about Bridgetown before.'

'Not even the Animal Flower cave?'

'Oh, that! You'd only be disappointed,' he said. 'It's full of worms. Granted they're spectacular because they are all the colours of the rainbow, but you'd be better at the museum where there are more civilised things to take up your attention. But that must be a decision for tomorrow,' he added, glancing at his watch. 'When you've had a word with your aunt we'll get back to the yacht club.'

For no very clear reason Andrina was thinking about them as a family paying a friendly call on a beloved relative before they returned to their own environment. Why? she wondered. Why?

Ward took Salty by the hand.

'We'll wait for you in the taxi,' he said.

Her aunt was studying her carefully as Andrina turned back on to the patio.

'He's being extremely kind,' she suggested. 'I can't think why.'

'Does he need to have an ulterior motive?' Andrina asked in a small, strangled voice.

'Gerry thinks so.' Belle was frowning. 'He doesn't trust him, and Ward has acted the pirate in the past, grabbing land where he could, apparently. Nettleton's belonged to his brother till Ward managed to get a share in it. Then, when Richard went off to get Nola out of his system, Ward took over entirely. That's as much as anyone knows,' she sighed. 'He doesn't encourage gossip.'

'I can tell you that he's working hard at Nettleton's to preserve it for Salty,' Andrina said. 'I believe that to be the truth, whatever bargain he came to with his brother, who seems to have run away from his responsibilities.'

'Gerry says he'll turn up, like the proverbial bad penny, when Ward least expects him, but I'm doubtful,' said Belle. 'He went off round the world, crewing for Jimmy Tissort on one of his spectacular sea adventures. Maybe one day he'll come back to Flambeau to write a book about it.'

'And Salty will have a real father, at last,' Andrina mused. 'Do you think that's what it's all about—Ward being responsible for her till Richard gets the accident out of his system?'

'It may well be,' Belle conceded. 'Apparently they were very close, as brothers sometimes are, and they no doubt think alike about the basic things in life.'

'Poor Salty!' Andrina said quietly.

'She appears to be perfectly happy,' Belle remarked. 'And very fond of you,' she added on a tentative note. 'But one day she'll have to have a formal education, here in Bridgetown or England.'

'Ward seems to dislike the idea at present, though he does recognise its inevitability,' Andrina said.

'I suppose you could help,' Belle reflected. 'The child has become very fond of you and she's never taken very kindly to discipline in the past.'

'Ward has allowed her to run wild.' Andrina walked to the edge of the patio. 'Do you want me to go back to Castaways to help Gerry?' she asked.

'I wish you would,' Belle sighed. 'I've always felt that he needs some sort of direction, although what I would have done without him when Albert died I don't know. I owe him so much, and Albert was very fond of him.'

Andrina nodded sympathetically.

'I know how it is,' she said. 'When we've—lost someone we loved very much it's a great comfort to have someone else to turn to who understands.'

'You really like Gerry?' Belle asked. 'He's a very happy person and I think he'd make you happy.'

Andrina stiffened at the suggestion.

'I'm not ready to be "made happy" in the way you mean, Aunt Belle,' she said. 'I'm not ready to marry anyone yet.'

'You've had a bad experience,' Belle agreed, 'but you'll fall in love again. Just you wait and see! You're young and attractive and you have plenty of time. But don't wait too long,' she cautioned. 'I'd like to see you comfortably settled.'

Andrina pulled her cotton shawl about her shoulders.

'When you come back to Castaways will be time enough,' she said.

Ward and Salty were waiting beside the taxi when she reached the dust road and Ward handed her into the front passenger seat. Salty squeezed in beside her, slipping a hot little hand into hers.

'You'll love the Animal Cave,' she said sleepily as they drove off in the direction of Bridgetown.

Ward smiled slightly in the darkness.

'Some people have a one-track mind!' he said.

Salty was sound asleep before they reached Carlisle Bay and ran down towards the Yacht Club. Between the Government Buildings and the Point the cliff sheltered dozens of small craft, but *Sea Hawk* stood out resplendently among them all, her tall masts touched by the glimmer of moonlight, her hull glistening in the light from the quay, and suddenly it was like coming home. It was the place where Ward wanted to be above all others. Andrina felt shaken by the knowledge that he had asked her to share this place with him, although it had only been from the exigency of the moment. Salty had need of her and he had given in to a childish whim.

When he had carried the sleeping child to her cabin amidships Andrina undressed her as best she could, pulling on her short pyjama trousers and a white cotton top which was much the worse for wear.

'She certainly does need clothes,' she said when Ward came below to look at them. 'She appears to have grown out of everything.'

'I'll show you to your cabin,' he said. 'Then perhaps you'd like a nightcap on deck. Cocoa—or something stronger?'

'Cocoa will be fine.' Andrina took a last look at Salty who did not even stir in her sleep. 'She doesn't appear to have a fever any more.'

'We'll check with the hospital, all the same,' he decided. 'You could ask about your aunt while we're there.'

'I'd thought of that. She gave me the consultant's name.'

He opened a door further along the corridor.

'You're in here,' he said. 'I hope you'll be comfortable.'

She had a vague idea that it was his own cabin and hesitated on the threshold.

'I'm putting you out,' she said. 'Something—smaller would have done.'

'The guest cabins have been stripped for some time,' he said. 'It's almost two years since I took out my last charter.'

'You miss all that,' she suggested.

'In a way, but I have no cause to grumble. One day I may go back to chartering, but not yet.'

Not till Salty was more or less off his hands!

Garson came along from the galley with a mug in each hand.

'I put rum in them, like you say, Mr Prentice,' he announced. 'It make you sleep good,' he added to Andrina as he handed her one of the mugs.

Ward took it from her.

'Up you go,' he said, nodding towards the companionway. 'I'll follow you with the cocoa.'

They sat out on the for'ard deck looking at the sea as the minutes ticked away and a great stillness descended on the Bay and on the town behind it. From a distance the sound of a steel band throbbed in the darkness among the trees, but near at hand there was only the slapping of the water on the schooner's hull to break the silence. Ward sat back with his elbows on the deck, content to look out and not to talk, and she sipped the hot cocoa, thinking how good it was to have not a care in the world.

That could be the effect of the rum, of course, the feeling of wellbeing it brought at the end of a busy day. Ward had no right to lace her drink with the white spirit of the Islands, but it certainly made her feel good.

But this isn't Ward, she thought in the next breath. It's merely a veneer used by the pirate in him to confuse me into accepting him for the time being.

Disturbed by the thought, she decided to go to bed.

'I'll turn in now, if you don't mind,' she said. 'We have rather a full day ahead of us tomorrow.'

He walked with her to the head of the companionway, glancing at the illuminated dial of his wrist-watch as if he thought it was far too early to end the day, but the prospect of the moon-blanched deck was far too dangerous for her to delay.

'Perhaps you'll give me a call in the morning,' she said.

'Salty will do that, I dare say,' he smiled. 'She's up at first light as a rule. Sleep well!'

The final, brief salute was completely formal and the wild beating of her heart subsided as she reached her cabin door.

Looking around, she was quickly aware that Ward had sacrificed his comfort for hers. The cabin was large and airy, with three portholes along each side and double bunks, one of which had been laid down for her use. There was a central table and another little chart table between the bunks, with a reading lamp placed strategically half-way so that it could be angled on either bunk as desired, and a selection of nautical books occupied the shelves below. Curiously Andrina read the titles, wondering about Ward's taste in literature, but really she might have guessed. With only one exception they were about the sea.

The volume which she recognised as different had no title on the spine, and when she took it out she realised that it was a diary, something so personal that even although she was now alone in the cabin, she replaced with haste. It seemed to have burned her fingers, for without a doubt all Ward's secret thoughts were sealed up there between its pages for his eyes alone.

Once she had got in between the crisp white cotton sheets she lay awake for a long time, wondering about the man who paced the deck above her and then seemed to settle down to look at the sea.

CHAPTER SIX

NEXT morning it was Salty who woke her, as Ward had predicted.

'We've all slept in,' she announced, 'but Ward says it doesn't matter because we're just going to the shops.' She paused to inspect Andrina's dressing-gown. 'That's pretty,' she observed. 'Did you buy it in Bridgetown?'

'No, in England. I've had it for a very long time. Perhaps we could get you one like it, though,' Andrina suggested.

'What would I use it for?' Salty wanted to know.

It was a difficult question to answer because she generally ran blithely into the garden in her night attire each morning and went straight to bed at night.

'It's a sort of coat to cover your pyjamas,' she explained, 'but perhaps we could leave it for a while. What would you like most?'

Salty evidently couldn't make up her mind.

'Something for the donkey,' she decided, at last.

'I meant for you to wear.'

'Oh! Well—trousers and things.'

'What about a pretty dress?'

'I'm not sure. They get in the way.' The blue eyes were gravely attentive as Andrina slipped into the green linen suit she had decided to wear for her first visit to Bridgetown. 'White gets dirty,' she pointed out helpfully.

'Not if you're just walking about, and it can easily be washed.'

'We could hang it over the boom,' Salty suggested, slipping off the other bunk where she had perched when she had first come in. 'That's where we dry our shirts.'

'Good!' Andrina smiled, picking up her handbag. 'Let's go!'

The pungent smell of frying bacon met them at the cabin door. At least they were not too late for breakfast.

Ward was at the toast-and-marmalade stage when they reached the saloon.

'I've overslept,' Andrina apologised. 'I'm sorry!'

'You were dead to the world when I looked in on you at seven o'clock,' he said briefly.

A deep flush spread into her cheeks. She hadn't thought to lock the cabin door.

'I'm generally awake by seven,' she explained, 'but I don't go to bed with a rum-laced drink as a rule!'

He laughed, serving them both with a portion of bacon and tomato straight from the frying-pan.

'Sorry we haven't any eggs,' he apologised.

'This is all I need.' It was amazing how hungry she felt after dining so well the evening before. 'When do the shops open?'

'Depending on what you're looking for, round about eight o'clock. Some of the more exclusive ones don't surface till ten.'

The morning was going to be fun, she thought, a surge of wellbeing rising to the surface as she buttered the slice of toast he handed her on a fork.

'Salty is toying with the idea of a dress,' she said, 'strictly for the grand occasion, you understand!'

'There are no "grand occasions" on Flambeau,' Ward assured her. 'Unless you intend to organise some social activity at Castaways—apart from the tourists.'

'It hadn't crossed my mind.' She bit into the thick toast. 'Don't you think it might spoil the general effect on an "island in the sun"?'

'I thought it might keep you amused,' he said, 'since you seem determined to stay.'

Andrina's smile vanished.

'I must stay, Ward, until I'm quite sure of the future as far as my aunt is concerned,' she said.

'You mean the treatment?' He sat down on the edge of the settee to finish his coffee. 'That will do her the world of good, apparently. She has every faith in it.'

'I must have a word with the specialist.' She finished the bacon, wiping her fingers on the paper napkin he had supplied. 'Then I'll feel more—secure.'

It was an odd word to use, but she could not imagine Flambeau without her aunt's reassuring presence in the background to give her confidence and the advice she would surely need.

'I'm ready!' Salty announced, wiping her lips with the back of her hand in true nautical fashion. 'C'mon!'

Ward handed her a paper napkin.

'They're much more ladylike,' he explained with a wry smile.

They walked the short distance from the Yacht Club to the town, breathing in the cool, salt-laden air as they turned up Bay Street towards Trafalgar Square. Salty was far more interested in the tall ships lining the wharf at the Careenage than she was in the prospect of buying clothes.

'Let's go and see who's here,' she suggested, tugging at Ward's sleeve, but he continued to guide her purposefully towards the town.

'Broad and Swan are the streets you'll probably want,' he suggested to Andrina. 'After that, I'll take you for some lunch and you can have a word with the specialist in the afternoon. I'll make the appointment for you when I make one for Salty. I don't want her to end up with a weak chest.'

The fact that he wasn't coming with them was faintly disappointing, but Andrina told herself that she could not expect him to go shopping for children's clothes. It was a woman's job. She could almost hear him saying so!

Salty skipped by her side.

'We could have an ice-cream somewhere,' she hinted. 'It wouldn't spoil our lunch.'

They turned the corner into Broad Street where the sun shone between the tall buildings, leaving one side in shadow and the other dazzlingly bright.

'We'll walk on the sunny side,' Salty decided when Ward had pointed out the club where he expected them to join him for lunch.

'Don't get too hot,' he cautioned, 'and buy a hat.'

Salty was swinging the bedraggled straw she wore on *Sea Hawk*, evidently loath to part with something she had owned for a very long time.

'Garson could bind it,' she pointed out, but Ward laughed the suggestion aside.

'I can afford a hat,' he decided, looking in his wallet which generally stuck out of the hip pocket of his faded jeans. 'You'll need some money,' he added, drawing out a sheaf of notes. 'You can bring back the change!'

For a reason she was unable to explain, Andrina felt acutely embarrassed. He had handed her a great deal of money, far more than she would need to equip Salty for Flambeau, but he evidently trusted her discretion.

'I won't spend this much,' she assured him, turning away.

It was such a domestic little scene, the man of the family making sure that his wife had sufficient for her needs, yet they were as far removed from that sort of intimacy as it was possible to be.

An odd constriction rose in her throat as she watched him stride away into Bolton Lane, a tall, arresting figure in his unfamiliar tropical suit, his proud head held unconsciously high as he crossed from one pavement to the other in search of the number he sought. Business as well as pleasure had brought him to Barbados and he was putting business first.

For an hour Andrina shepherded Salty from one shop to the next, aware that the child was completely indifferent to clothes but determined to perform this service for Ward to the best of her ability. Pyjamas were a must, then some underwear, which Salty thought superfluous, and finally, when vivid red and yellow jeans had been added to the pile together with some matching T-shirts, she suggested a suitable dress.

Salty heaved a deep sigh.

'All right,' she agreed guardedly, 'but I don't want a long skirt.'

'Of course not! Whatever put that idea into your head?' Andrina asked.

'You see them in the magazines—kids in long dresses. They look silly,' Salty declared. 'People leave magazines on *Sea Hawk* when we charter her,' she explained.

'All right, we won't buy a long dress,' Andrina agreed. 'Not this time.'

They discovered a likely boutique in Swan Street where the proprietress understood the reluctant child. Salty wandered about the shop showing very little interest at first, but finally her eyes lit on a skirt and jacket which had a matching blouse.

'That one,' she decided, fingering the fine *broderie anglaise* at the hem and cuffs. 'It has lots and lots of holes in it!'

Andrina laughed as she exchanged glances with the proprietress.

'A good enough recommendation, I suppose,' she suggested, aware that Salty had chosen well if a little expensively. 'Now, perhaps a cotton dress for second-best and we're through.'

While a young assistant searched along a nearby rail she was suddenly aware of an audience and turned quickly to find Ward standing in the doorway. For a moment his expression was baffling, a mixture of the old amusement and something that was almost pain as he watched Salty struggle into a checked gingham pinafore with a white pleated 'bib' at the neck which she evidently admired.

'I suppose you'd call that "shocking pink",' he said in the next instant, the smile deepening around his mouth although the shadow of pain remained in his eyes. 'Have you everything you want?'

There were shoes and a tiny handbag to go with the white suit.

'Do you think they're quite Salty?' he asked, but Salty had taken a fancy to the handbag, at least. 'Parcel them up,' he told the waiting assistant. 'We really do need an ice-cream now!'

When their purchases had been tied with multi-coloured tape and handed over to Andrina he relieved her of her burden, passing a large carrier bag to his niece.

'Something for the donkey,' he explained.

Salty peeped inside.

'Carrots!' she exclaimed. 'And something else.' Suddenly her eyes were shining. 'A new harness! It's absolutely what he needs most of all!'

They walked, laughing, to the nearest ice-cream parlour and then to the Careenage to see the ships lying alongside until it was time to go to Ward's club for lunch. Salty became more subdued as she went through the swing doors, but gave her order for coo-coo with flying-fish with an adult dignity which delighted the waiter, who knew her from previous visits. Ward drank his rum 'straight up' but ordered fruit punches for his guests.

'You're being very kind,' said Andrina, meeting his eyes with a new light in her own.

'Why not?' he demanded. 'You've done me a favour and I must try to repay it as best I can.'

Was that all? Was he entertaining her merely out of gratitude because she had taken a difficult task off his hands for half a day, and would he forget her memorable experience as soon as they sailed away from Bridgetown in the morning?

Yes, of course he would. She was merely an instrument of convenience where Ward Prentice was concerned—although she had surprised a strange look of pain in his eyes as he had watched them from the boutique doorway.

Why did she care so much? Why did the thought of his indifference hurt? Had she been mad enough to fall in love for a second time with a man who could only bring her torture and pain?

Turning to the window, she looked down on the busy street below, on the crowd of happy people walking in the sunshine and on the sun itself dappling the pavements with light and shade, like life, she thought. Being glad one minute and sad the next.

'I've had a happy day and my heart is singing,' Salty announced. 'Is your heart happy, Andrina?'

Ward looked across the table, waiting for her answer.

'Very happy,' she said, wondering if she lied.

Her afternoon was entirely taken up by her visit to the hospital while Ward took Salty off to a child care clinic where he had made an appointment with a friend who was a clever paediatrician. When they met again in Roebuck Street, as arranged, they had good news to exchange.

'Salty passed all the tests with honour,' Ward declared. 'How about your aunt?'

'She has to stay for treatment till the end of the month,' Andrina reported, 'but after that she should be well on the way to recovery.'

'And back at Flambeau,' he mused. 'It calls for a celebration, don't you think?'

'I think we should go back to St Thomas or Aunt Belle will be wondering what kept us so late,' Andrina suggested. 'I don't really want to tell her that I've seen her specialist—it's rather like spying on her—but I do want her to know about Castaways, that she'll come back there and everything will be the same as before.'

'With Fabian and you waiting for her on the doorstep?'

She flushed sensitively.

'I suppose that was what I meant,' she said as Salty rushed ahead of them towards the taxi-rank.

'Are you going to marry Fabian?' he asked bluntly.

'Why should I?' she countered. 'But if my aunt is going to be away for a month we'll have to work together.'

'See that he pulls his weight, in that case,' he advised bluntly. 'All that land above Castaways could be utilised to grow crops for the hotel, even if you don't want to market them.'

'Why are you suggesting all this when you know you want the land for yourself?' she asked unhappily.

He hailed a taxi.

'Because I hate to see land being wasted,' he growled. 'Your aunt has refused to sell me the land on Fabian's advice——'

'And you've decided to work on me,' she supplied, looking him straight in the eye as he held open the taxi door. 'I'm completely inexperienced, Ward, but I see no reason why I should go against my aunt's wishes. She doesn't want to sell, so neither would I.'

'Which is fair enough,' he agreed with maddening magnanimity. 'So can we forget about Flambeau and what I would like to do for it and just be friends?'

'You've made that difficult——'

'But on second thoughts you might consider it?'

Did he know how demanding he could be? she wondered. Did he know how she felt about him, deep down in her heart? As he closed the taxi door firmly behind Salty she tried to tell herself that he was not to be trusted but could not. Arrogant, even harsh he might be, but he had managed to touch her heart, if only where Salty was concerned and she did respect him now.

Perhaps that was how it would always be between them. Respect and trust, but nothing more.

It was a short enough drive to St Thomas, but an eternity seemed to have passed before they reached their destination. I'm in love with him, she thought. It seems as if I've been in love with Ward for ever.

CHAPTER SEVEN

THEY set sail for Flambeau early the following morning after spending what Andrina could only think of as a 'family evening' at her aunt's hotel.

Anxious not to repeat the distressing experience of the limbo dancing, Ward had readily accepted Belle's invitation to share a meal with her on the patio of her apartment, and Salty had unpacked their purchases for her aunt's approval, even to the carrots and the new harness for the donkey which was no doubt her greatest treasure. Belle had admired the white suit with the finely-pleated pink blouse and Salty had said quite solemnly that she would keep it till her father came home.

One glance at Ward's face had shown Andrina the same look which she had surprised in his eyes as he had watched them from the boutique doorway, while Belle had taken Salty on to her ample knee to hug her close and say that it was 'a very good idea'.

When *Sea Hawk* sailed back across Carlisle Bay it was hardly light, but Andrina knew that Ward had been on deck for most of the starlit hours, pacing up and down with that same look in his eyes, thinking about the past.

The aroma of frying bacon met her as she opened her cabin door, the familiar smell which always heralded a new day.

'I can't possibly be late this morning,' she said as Ward came into view at the head of the companionway. 'Have you been up all night?'

Immediately she asked the question she regretted it, remembering the pacing footsteps along the deck.

'More or less,' he admitted briefly, 'but loss of sleep hardly worries me. It happens all the time on a ship like *Sea Hawk*, as you'll appreciate if we have a storm.'

He had brushed her concern for him aside, answering her as the mariner rather than the man, making her feel acutely conscious of intrusion.

'I could easily have occupied another cabin and given you your own,' she pointed out. 'The one next to Salty's would have done very well.'

'It wouldn't have made any difference,' he said. 'I often sleep on deck.' They had reached the saloon and he ushered her in. 'I hope the smell of frying bacon increases your appetite,' he added lightly. 'It's our regular menu when we're at sea.'

'Garson cooks very well,' she agreed. 'Does he help at Nettleton's, too?'

Again she was conscious of prying into his immediate background, but he answered her readily enough.

'He's second-in-command to Berthe,' he said. 'When you have a good native housekeeper you don't interfere. You let her have full control of the domestic staff, at least. Only the lady of the house can give her orders. Berthe is a proud and loyal servant so, fundamentally, I want for nothing.'

Except a wife, Andrina thought, a mistress for Nettleton's, someone to take Nola's place, although perhaps that was impossible. Once Ward had loved completely there would be no room for second best. Perhaps only for Salty's sake would he consider marriage now. Had he made that clear from the beginning, she wondered, unable to imagine him changing his mind.

They spent the remainder of the voyage on deck, sprawled out in the sun or sheltered from it by the canvas awning which Garson erected over the well at midday so that they could eat in the open. It was an idyllic situation, with time suspended as they drove through the blue water before a gentle trade wind, and they lay back to enjoy it, gazing up through the rigging at the spread of brown sail filling with the wind and the cloudless sky beyond. Conversation seemed of little importance as they sped along with only the rush of the waves against the hull to break the vast silence of the seas, and suddenly Andrina felt that

she could go on like this for ever, with no questions asked
or answered. In his true element, which was the sea, Ward
was an ideal companion, wanting nothing more than a
pipeful of tobacco to smoke with his back propped against
a mast and his long legs stretched out on the deck, asking
nothing but the infinite tranquillity of the ocean where the
silver flying-fish darted ahead of *Sea Hawk*, joyous in the
sun.

When, finally, Flambeau took shape on the horizon she
felt a deep regret, but all perfect things had to come to an
end sooner or later, she supposed.

Ward steered the schooner in between the reefs and the
anchor chain rattled down into the green water of the
lagoon, shattering its peace. They could see Gerry standing
on the jetty, obviously waiting for their return.

'Garson will put you ashore,' said Ward, all the easy-
going indulgence gone from his voice. 'I hope everything
has been running smoothly while you've been away.'

'It was only for two days,' Andrina said. 'Surely nothing
drastic could have happened in such a short time.'

Disappointed that Garson had been singled out to see her
safely to the jetty, she turned to say goodbye to Salty.

'I wish you were coming back to Nettleton's with us,' the
child said generously, putting thin arms about her neck. 'I
love you very much!'

It was almost more than Andrina could do to keep the
tears out of her eyes, yet she managed a reassuring smile.

'Perhaps Ward will allow you to ride over to Castaways
more often,' she suggested. 'Then we could swim in the
lagoon.'

Ward helped Garson to lower the tender and then
handed her in. The few purchases she had made on her own
account were in a red plastic carrier bag which he passed to
her without comment, watching as Garson dipped his oars
into the pellucid water for the short journey to the shore.
Before they had reached the jetty he had turned away, but
Salty stood on the for'ard deck in a pair of her new jeans
waving frantically till her arms must have been tired.

Gerry stooped to catch the mooring rope which Garson threw to him.

'Welcome home!' he said. 'Did you have a good trip?'

He seemed to be full of a new confidence, waiting for her to ask about Castaways, but she answered his question first.

'Barbados was a revelation to me. I had no idea Bridgetown was so attractive. My aunt is much better, too, but it will take another month of treatment before she's really fit. After that she should be quite able to cope. She looked well and seemed to be comfortably settled at St Thomas.'

'That's fine,' he nodded, untying the painter to push the tender off. 'You haven't much luggage.'

'I only bought a few essentials,' she explained. 'Most of the time I shopped for Salty.' She felt curiously disinclined to discuss her trip in depth. 'How's the water supply?' she asked, remembering how short they had been before she had left for Barbados.

'Much improved.' Gerry gave her a sideways glance. 'When it comes to the crunch I would say it was Nature's gift to the island.'

She turned to look at him.

'What do you mean by that?' she asked, a flutter of apprehension rising in her throat.

'Well, one for all and all for one. Prentice has no real authority when it comes to controlling the main supply.'

She felt as if she was rooted to the spot.

'Gerry, you haven't tampered with Ward's spring?' she gasped. 'The water he needs for Nettleton's?'

'Not to any great extent.' He said it carelessly. 'He has more water than he can possibly use.'

'That's not the point!' She felt the cold conviction of Ward's anger settling on her heart. 'We each have our separate springs and we can't argue if Ward's is the more reliable.'

He put an arm about her shoulders.

'We don't use very much,' he said.

Andrina bit her lip.

'We have no right to use Nettleton's water at all,' she pointed out. 'If we only had a trickle that would be enough.'

'You forget we're trying to run a hotel,' he said.

'We must try to economise.'

'You try telling that to our guests. We've got a right lot this time——baths every day and constant changes of water in the pool.'

They had reached the clearing in the trees where the freshwater pool lay dazzlingly blue in the bright sunlight.

'It will have to do for the time being,' she said.

'We can't deprive people of a swim.'

'They can take it in the lagoon. If they're too lazy to walk down to the beach that's just too bad. We drain the pool every day. Just think of the extra water we must use!'

'I did give it some thought,' Gerry agreed, 'but I can't see why Prentice should have all the privileges. However, let's forget about it and tell me what you did in Bridgetown.'

Andrina could not think of Bridgetown without remembering Ward and Salty and how happy they had been in her company, but now she had to think about Gerry and what he had done to the water supply.

'When you said "not to any great extent" about the water what did you mean?' she asked.

'I dug a little channel from his spring down to our outlet. Nothing much, just enough to keep us ticking over till our supply fills up again. We haven't had any rain for weeks, but I heard a rumble of thunder yesterday, so we may be lucky,' he decided.

'I hope you're right,' said Andrina, although she could not help worrying about the diverted water. 'You should have asked Ward first.'

'How could I do that when he was escorting you round Bridgetown?' he demanded. 'But if you insist I'll see him in a day or two.'

'I wish you would,' Andrina said uneasily.

Ward came to Castaways, however, long before Gerry

remembered to visit Nettleton's. He rode in on Simon, tethering the red stallion to a post before he strode purposefully towards the house. It was the afternoon rest hour and most of the guests were in their chalets or down on the beach stretched out on the cane loungers beneath the palms. It was very hot.

Andrina saw him coming from her verandah and her heart seemed to miss a beat. There was no mistaking his mood.

'Where's Fabian?' he asked when she went to meet him.

'He's down at the lagoon.' She looked up into his dark face. 'Ward, if you've come about the water, I'm sorry. I don't suppose Gerry thought too carefully when he tampered with it.'

'Thought!' he exclaimed. 'Anyone would have *known* you couldn't dig a trench that deep without diverting half of my supply to your own use. If you'd wanted water for drinking or cooking that would have been a different matter, but what you're using in your swimming-pool for your guests' pleasure is Nettleton's life's blood. I don't suppose you would have thought of that, since you appear to have a one-track mind.'

She drew back, stung by the injustice of his accusation.

'You've every right to be angry,' she allowed, 'but I had no idea how much water we've been using. I thought it was no more than a trickle.'

'Fabian probably told you that.' Some of the anger had died out of his eyes. 'I should have realised it was done while we were in Barbados, but Nettleton's means a great deal to me. I can't stand aside and see it go under for want of irrigation. I've filled in the trench and I hope you won't be too inconvenienced, but I can't divert much-needed water into your pipeline for a swimming-pool. Your guests will have to make do with the lagoon, which is better for them, anyway.'

Andrina's own reaction had been much the same, but two days had elapsed since she had made the observation to Gerry on the evening of their return from Bridgetown, and that was a long time to drain water from an illicit source.

'I should have come to you at once,' she said. 'I'm sorry, Ward, but I had no idea it was so serious.'

He turned on his heel, ashamed of his initial anger.

'I shouldn't have bawled you out like that,' he said, 'but it seemed such a senseless thing to do.'

'It was, and you had every right to be angry. We don't really need a freshwater pool,' she said. 'It's a luxury.'

'What about your domestic supply?'

'We must cut down on that—baths and things.'

'There's no need. I've left you a narrow outlet to your storage tank on the hill,' he explained. 'That should do till your spring fills up again.'

'Gerry says he heard thunder recently—the day we came back,' she remembered.

His expression sharpened as he looked up at the mountain.

'It could have been,' he agreed. 'We must certainly hope so.'

'Do you think it might have been—the mountain?' Her heart was clamped in a sudden knot of fear. 'Gerry described it as a rumble—like thunder.'

'No doubt he was right.' Ward untied Simon from the post. 'There's been nothing since.'

Before he mounted she said:

'Surely you'll stay for something to drink? It's very warm.'

He hesitated, looking up towards the mountain for a second time.

'I must get back to Nettleton's straight away. I have a lot to do. I'm sorry if I sounded too severe just now,' he added, 'but water means a great deal to us on the other side of the ridge.'

'We were at fault,' Andrina acknowledged, watching as he swung into the saddle. 'I don't think Gerry really meant to be awkward. It was just that——'

He waited for her to finish, not helping her with her excuse for Gerry's conduct.

'He just didn't think,' she concluded lamely.

He reined the stallion's head round to face the mountain.

'If there should be an emergency you'd better come to me,' he said briefly.

'Ward——'

He turned in the saddle to look at her, his eyes half closed against the sun.

'Thank you for Barbados,' she managed. 'I really did enjoy myself.'

His grim mouth relaxed in a smile.

'Salty is very grateful,' he said. 'She's tried on the gingham dress several times to look at herself in the mirror!'

'And the white suit?'

His eyes clouded.

'She's keeping that for a special occasion.'

'For her father's return. Do you expect your brother to come back soon?'

Waiting for his answer to what he might consider an impertinent question, she realised that Richard's return to Nettleton's could mean his own release. He would be free then to go back to his roving existence aboard *Sea Hawk* instead of being tied to an estate which needed constant supervision to survive.

'I haven't heard from Richard for six months,' he said, 'but that's perhaps understandable. He couldn't settle after Nola died and Nettleton's was a constant reminder to him, but one day I hope he'll come, for Salty's sake. An uncle is a poor substitute for a father, as you've already pointed out.'

'I didn't mean to criticise you unduly,' Andrina apologised. 'It was unforgivable, since I really didn't know you at the time.'

He looked down at her from Simon's back.

'Do you know me now, Andrina?' he asked.

'I hope I do.' Suddenly her voice faltered. 'We got off on the wrong foot in the beginning.'

He laughed abruptly.

'It's easy to do,' he said. 'Tell Fabian I'll guarantee him

enough water so long as he doesn't tamper with the springs.'

He rode off before she could thank him.

'What was all that about?' Gerry asked, coming up from the lagoon. 'Was Prentice here to bawl us out about the water supply?'

'Can you blame him?' Andrina had to make an effort to keep her anger in check. 'If you'd only gone to him in the first place and *asked* he wouldn't have denied us reasonable access to his spring. He said so, but naturally he was annoyed when you took the law into your own hands and diverted too much water from Nettleton's. He's made provision for us now with an adequate supply into our storage tank.'

'So all's well that ends well!' He kissed her perfunctorily on the cheek as his arm went round her waist. 'How about a swim to cool down?' he suggested. 'I've never known it quite so hot.'

She glanced up towards the mountain where a man on horseback had paused on the high dust road behind Castaways, but whether Ward was looking down on them or up at the twin peaks was difficult to surmise. Almost subconsciously she moved out of Gerry's embrace.

'The swim will have to wait,' she decided. 'I've a menu to work out for tonight's dinner and someone suggested a visit to the spice groves for tomorrow. You could arrange that, Gerry. You could ask Ward.'

'And be met with a blank refusal? I don't relish going cap-in-hand to Nettleton's at the present moment.'

'I'm quite sure he wouldn't refuse,' said Andrina. 'Aunt Belle has been sending her guests over there for a long time, I understand. Please see to it.'

It was the first time she had used her authority and she was immediately aware of Gerry's resentment.

'I'll do my best,' he said dryly. 'Trust me!'

Andrina turned in the direction of the kitchen, thinking that she was making a poor attempt at managing Castaways, but she could only do her best, as Gerry had just remarked.

CHAPTER EIGHT

FOR the next few days the heat was almost insufferable, a tense, still heat which seemed unnatural in this subtropical paradise where the trade winds tempered everything to perfection. The wind, when it did blow, brought no immediate release from the furnace-like conditions, and once or twice there was a murmur like thunder in the distance but still no rain.

Their guests grew restless, complaining most of the time. They were especially critical of the lack of water in the swimming-pool and the restrictions on daily baths. It wasn't what they had paid for, and although Andrina did her best to explain about the springs, there was a great deal of criticism from the types who had booked to come to Castaways for the wrong reasons. Everything in the romantic garden had to be wonderful and when Castaways fell short of perfection they were aggrieved.

'You can't please 'em all,' Gerry said philosophically. 'You have to take the rough with the smooth.'

'Perhaps when the thunder breaks things will be better,' Andrina said. 'I heard another peel this morning, but it seemed far away. Almost underground,' she added speculatively.

'I wouldn't discount the mountain,' Gerry mused. 'It has been known to "grumble" off and on over a period of years. The natives fear it, of course, talking of devils, and some of them remember it "spewing up", as they so elegantly put it, several years ago. About ten, I think.'

'You're not suggesting a sudden eruption?'

He shook his head.

'No way. There'd be other signs.'

'Such as?'

'Warning spouts, I've heard them called—short out-

bursts of flame with lava and rocks spewing a little way
down the mountainside, or maybe an earth tremor or two.'

'What about the "thunder"?' she asked.

'The mountain has always grumbled a bit.'

'Shouldn't we take some sort of precaution?' she suggested.

'I've arranged that. We can get anything of value into the
launch and make for Grenada in an hour. As for our guests,'
he shrugged, 'we can arrange to have them collected from
the other side. But really,' he added with supreme opti-
mism, 'you have no need to worry. It may never happen.'

'Ward offered his help,' she said, remembering his exact
words. 'He said we could go to him in an emergency.'

'He'll have plenty to do to look after Nettleton's and the
villages,' Gerry said. 'If the mountain erupts the lava will
come down on his side of the ridge, as it did before.'

'It will destroy all he's built up,' said Andrina under her
breath. 'It will be a terrible blow to him.'

'Devastating,' Gerry agreed, 'since he's built it all up
practically from scratch, his own little kingdom which he
no doubt hopes to rule for ever.'

'That's not quite true,' she objected with growing conviction. 'He was doing it mostly for Salty and the people of
Flambeau. He believes his brother will come back one of
these days to take over his half-share in Nettleton's.'

'Richard?' Gerry smiled. 'Prentice is batting on a sticky
wicket if he believes that. Richard has made his escape and
wild horses won't drive him back.'

'What about Salty?'

'Salty might be a problem. My guess is that he'll collect
her and vanish, leaving Prentice to do what he likes with
Nettleton's and most of the island.'

It was a harsh assessment, and suddenly Andrina knew
how jealous Gerry was. What Ward was doing at Nettleton's was something he admired, something he might have
achieved for himself but for the streak of indolence in his
nature which he could not eradicate, and so he sought to
denigrate the other man's success in belittling words and

paltry actions which seemed to prove his own ability, such as getting the water for the hotel and making his individual arrangements for evacuating Castaways.

As the heat intensified and a copper-coloured cloud hovered over the mountain Andrina's anxiety grew. Among the hotel guests tempers became increasingly frayed, while the Caribs looked constantly towards the horizon for the expected wind, their dark eyes reflecting their natural fear, since most of them had seen it all before.

'There goin' to be one big helluva blow,' Pete predicted, his dark eyes rolling in his head. 'I never seen it so still. Even de cockatoos don't screech no more.'

Andrina had noticed the increasing silence of the caged birds, and the flight southwards of a whole flock of birds had darkened the sky the day before, a sure sign that nature herself was uneasy.

The first definite warning came from the mountain itself, a deep-throated rumbling which sent Luella and Pete scurrying for shelter under the kitchen table. When it did not repeat itself after an hour they emerged, looking decidedly sheepish.

'That ol' devil mountain he jus' got one big belly-ache!' Luella decided. 'He no' blow at all!'

There were signs of more activity by nightfall, however. What could not be seen in the bright light of day became painfully obvious when the sky grew dark. The orange glow beneath the cloud was seen as a halo of flame on the mountain's brow and intermittent spurts of fire shot up from the crater far below. Of course, it had happened before; of course, the mountain had grumbled, but only for a day or two, after which it had subsided peacefully for years.

This, however, seemed to be different. There was a subdued restlessness everywhere, with the faintest smell of sulphur in the air, and the guests' complaining gave Andrina the kind of headache she scarcely ever experienced. An iron band seemed to be tightly clamped over her brow, while her eyelids felt as if they were weighted with lead.

She spent a sleepless night tossing in the humid atmosphere between sheets which were already soaked with perspiration and at daybreak was standing in her nightdress, barefooted, on her patio when the first plume of black smoke rose straight up from the nearest peak. The mountain was about to erupt.

Her first sensation was fear, and then she found herself walking quietly in the direction of Gerry's room. He was awake and standing beside the window as if completely fascinated by what he saw.

'We'll have to get the guests away,' she said as calmly as she could.

'The guests?' He turned to look at her almost in bewilderment. 'It's happened, you see,' he said. 'The sort of thing you dread but never quite believe in. We're going to be sealed off here, like rats in a trap!'

'Don't talk nonsense!' She swallowed her own fear. 'But it's a warning and we'll have to get these people over to Grenada in case—in case it really is a blow. You can take them over in the launch as soon as they've packed their cases and we'll see how things are when you come back.'

'Come back?' he echoed. 'You must be joking! When we go over there you're coming with us. Don't make a fuss about it,' he added darkly. 'I'm not letting you take any risks. We're going together—now, as soon as I can get the launch.'

'*You're* going, Gerry,' she said quietly. 'You and the other guests, but I mean to stay. Even if the mountain does blow it won't be over in a second, I understand, and Ward may need help. There's all the children in the village to consider, and the scattered settlements in the hills.'

'Prentice has his minions on the estate to look after all that. They're not our responsibility.'

'They're Ward's, and I'm going to help.'

'You'll get precious little thanks for your trouble,' he warned. 'Drina, be sensible and come to Grenada. We'll be there in under an hour. We'll be safe.'

She looked at him as if she were seeing him for the first time.

'I couldn't—run away,' she said quietly. 'Not in any circumstance.'

'You're mad!' He caught her bare arm. 'Do you want to die?'

'Not any more than you do, but I know I can't go now when we have no word of—the others.'

'You mean Prentice, of course,' he said viciously. 'Well, good luck to you! I just hope he can get you off in time. This island's going to go up as if a bomb had been put under it, and you'll go with it if you don't come to your senses. I'll give you half an hour to think about it,' he said as he clambered into his trousers. 'It's all I'm going to give the others.'

Andrina watched him go in a sort of trance, not quite believing that he was about to abandon Castaways at the first suggestion of danger, then she hurried towards the kitchen where Luella and Pete were cowering behind the door, eyes rolling as a tremendous rattle descended from the mountain.

Looking out through the window, she saw a column of ash and fire rising from the second peak to descend in a gigantic pyrotechnic display, like a waterfall cascading down the mountainside. L'Anse Deux Feux, she thought. The beach on Ward's side of the island had been aptly named!

'Luella, make sandwiches,' she instructed with amazing calm. 'Anything will do. And you, Pete, go up to Nettleton's and ask Mr Prentice if there's anything you can do. He may want to bring the hill people down to the village.'

'No, ma'am!' said Pete, shaking his head. 'I go by the beach. No way I go near dat mountain when he spittin' fire in me face!'

'Go whichever way you choose,' Andrina said, 'so long as you get there. Unless,' she added, 'you mean to run away.'

Pete straightened his bent shoulders.

'You no' run, I no' run,' he said, glaring defiantly at the

vivid sky. 'All de devils on de mountain no' make me run if
yo' stay!'

Luella nodded in agreement.

'Me, too!' she said. 'I stay with you an' Mr Prentice.
He know what to do. Sure he know!'

The guests assembled in the main hall quietly enough
with their belongings in a heap on the floor beside them.
Some of them wanted to stay, but Gerry soon persuaded
them into the launch with the assurance that Grenada
would be safer for them for a day or two.

'If you're worrying about paying for a holiday you
haven't had,' he joked, 'I'm sure you'll be able to claim a
refund!'

There was a certain amount of nervous laughter as they
filed down to the beach, and he turned to look at Andrina.

'You're being a fool,' he said. 'Anything could happen.'

'I think I'm aware of that,' she assured him quietly.
'Goodbye, Gerry, and if we don't meet again, good luck!'

He stood gazing at her for a moment longer.

'You'll regret this silly demonstration of fidelity,' he
said. 'Change your mind now and come with us.'

She shook her head.

'My mind is quite made up.'

He stooped to kiss her, but she evaded his lips, his part-
ing caress falling on her cheek.

'Be careful, Gerry,' she said. 'If you get to Barbados
will you go and see my aunt?'

'She won't be too happy about this,' he warned.

'I think she'll understand,' Andrina said, turning back
towards the house.

She forced herself not to look at the mountain, but the
vivid glow above it had coloured the whole sky. The noise
from the hidden crater increased as the hours slipped away
and she tried to involve Luella in the ordinary domestic
tasks of their busy day. Pete had gone in search of Ward,
making his way farther south along the beach before he
turned inland towards Nettleton's. It was a longer route,
but it avoided the ridge where the mountain had spewed

out its wrath during a former eruption and it gave him the courage he needed. Josh had gone with Gerry to help with the launch, but he had promised to come back.

At about two o'clock a slight tremor shook Castaways to its foundations and then all the lamps and crockery righted themselves and there was no more sound.

How long would it take Pete to reach Nettleton's? Andrina pondered the question, wondering if Ward would come right away. She realised that he would have his own plans made for Nettleton's which might not include Castaways, and the thought made her glance swiftly in the direction of the mountain which continued to belch black smoke from one crater and fire from the other. Sometimes it subsided, but only to gather renewed momentum for a further explosion. None of them were severe; only frightening in their suggestion of destructive power, but she found herself looking towards the dust road with growing apprehension.

When Ward did come she was taken almost by surprise. He rode down between the trees on Simon, his hand tight-clenched on the rein, and before he slid from the saddle she recognised the telltale marks of strain on his face. His eyes when he looked at her were dark with anxiety.

'I need your help,' he said. 'Salty has disappeared.'

She ran towards him.

'Where—when?'

'An hour ago.' His voice was tense. 'She rode out on the donkey, but it came back without her.' He glanced at the mountain. 'We've no way of telling where she went, but the odds are that she's had an accident. I've searched along the shore and Garson has been to the village, but there's no sign of her.'

'Have you tried the mountain road?' she suggested. 'The road over the ridge. She could have been coming here.'

He shook his head, a small pulse hammering at his temple.

'I don't think so. In an odd sort of way she feared the mountain, maybe because she listened to the Carib superstitions about it.' His jaw tightened. 'They're nonsense, of course, but to a small child they could be very real. Salty is precious to me, Andrina. I made my brother a promise to look after her.'

Andrina's heart contracted with a new kind of pain.

'She was there, in New York, when her mother died, wasn't she?'

He nodded, preparing to remount the stallion to continue his search.

'Yes.' His eyes were on the far horizon. 'I brought her back to Flambeau. She was with Nola in an upstairs bedroom when the fire started, but someone threw her out of the hotel window.'

Andrina could see it all so vividly, and the impression such an experience would leave on the mind of an intelligent child like Salty.

'She could have been upset by the sight of the volcano.' She put a detaining hand on Ward's stirrup. 'Deux Feux,' she added tensely. 'Two fires! Did she see them from your side of the ridge and panic?'

'I thought about that, but she would have come home, in that case.' Ward drew a deep breath, already digging his heels into the stallion's flank. 'That's why I'm convinced there must have been an accident.'

'Let me help,' she offered. 'Let me come with you.'

He glanced over her head towards the hotel.

'You'll have enough to do here if the mountain does blow,' he told her. 'It's my opinion it will go on our side of the ridge, but it's really anyone's guess. Where's Fabian?' His brows creased into a dark line.

'He—took everyone off to Grenada this morning.'

There was a pause in which his opinion of Gerry was reflected plainly in his eyes.

'I suppose he wanted you to go, too,' he said between his teeth. 'Why didn't you?'

She could have told him the truth in that moment. She could have said 'because I love you with all my heart and always will', but instead she let go of the stirrup so that he could ride away whenever he wanted to.

'I didn't think things were bad enough,' she said instead. 'I considered I had a duty to Castaways while my aunt was away.'

He looked at her in silence for a moment.

'There could be danger,' he admitted. 'If the mountain goes up in smoke the lava flow could trap you as easily as it could destroy the harbour and the villages on my side of the ridge. You should have taken the opportunity to go with Fabian.'

She shook her head.

'I'm staying,' she said stubbornly. 'You're going to need help, if it's only to look for Salty.'

He thought for a moment longer.

'Take the Moke and get Luella and the others to Nettleton's,' he commanded. 'We're on high ground over there and I mean to evacuate the villages and the harbour area. If it's destroyed at least the fishermen and their families will be safe.'

'All you've done,' she said sympathetically. 'Surely it won't go like that!'

He shrugged, pulling Simon's head round to take the steep slope to the dust road.

'The Caribs come first. Do as I say about Nettleton's. Get your people up there.'

'Ward——!' she called as he rode away, but he did not seem to hear.

She had alerted Luella to the possibility of evacuation when she suddenly thought of Salty. If the child had been afraid, if she had taken the donkey along the beach at L'Anse Deux Feux, she could have panicked at sight of the belching smoke and fire from the mountain, turning back in fear to gallop the donkey too fast along the beach, or the little animal could have bolted and thrown her. But Ward said that he had already searched the beach, finding nothing.

Suddenly she remembered Salty's 'secret place', the cave where the child had said she went but which nobody knew about. 'Except you,' she had said, pointing vaguely in the direction of the mountain. Yet would she have gone there when she was so afraid of fire? The twin peaks had already been belching smoke and flame when she had set out and she would have seen them from the beach. But not if she had come through the spice grove on her way to Castaways. Only as she crossed the ridge would Salty have seen the volcanoes.

Andrina called to Luella to be quick.

'We'll go to Nettleton's straight away,' she said. 'I have to find Mr Prentice.'

'You no' find him hiding up there at Nettleton's,' Luella assured her with conviction. 'Mr Prentice, he be all over de island savin' folk from dat ol' mountain an' all de fire devils who live there. You jus' take my word for it, Miss Drina. He work hisself to a standstill to save dem people on de estate an' all de little chil'ren down at de harbour.' Her black eyes were suddenly full of horror. 'De harbour she be blown away,' she mourned. 'Der be no mor' wall after de wave come.'

Was there always a tidal wave after an eruption, Andrina wondered, and would it completely wreck Ward's half-finished harbour? All he had done, all he had promised himself, might be swept away in a few terrifying minutes of utter fury and he would be left with nothing. Yet he would not sail away on *Sea Hawk*, as he might have done, protecting himself at Flambeau's expense.

She set her teeth in swift determination. That was why her place was here beside him, whether he wanted her or not.

When she had started up the mini-moke she packed a few possessions into it and one or two things she knew were precious to her aunt, like the portrait of Albert Speitz which hung on her sitting-room wall and the small portmanteau where she kept her personal papers and a few trinkets which spelled out a lifetime of loving and giving. The cockatoos and the little parrot were hastily transferred to wicker cages which usually housed the domestic poultry when they were replenished from Grenada and the mini-moke was more than full once she had settled Luella in the back seat with the livestock. There had been no sign of the launch returning, but she thought Josh would bring it back. Perhaps Gerry would change his mind and come back, too, but she did not really think he would. Utterly selfish, he had abandoned Castaways without a second thought, putting his own immediate interests before her aunt's. I could never have married him, she thought.

The mini-moke was old. It took the steep incline to the dirt road reluctantly but seemed to pick up strength once it had crossed the ridge and turned in at the entrance to Nettleton's. Andrina had kept her eyes averted when the mountain had come in sight, but she could not shut out the hot, sulphurous smell and the stillness over everything. It was as if the twin peaks were waiting to trap them as they would trap the villages and the harbour where the fishermen's cottages clustered along the shore.

Torn between going directly in search of Salty and her responsibility for Luella, who was old and afraid, she decided to seek out Ward first. I need his advice and some of his strength, she thought.

The scent of spice was strong in the air as they went down into the grove, as if the silent trees were attempting to combat the sulphurous breath of the volcano, but here and there they crackled with the heat, their leaves already limp even in the shade. Nettleton's seemed a long way away, and suddenly Andrina realised that there was no birdsong. Salty's birds had either flown away or were cowering in the undergrowth in the unaccustomed heat.

The stillness seemed to increase as they drew nearer to the house, but suddenly there was the sound of an approaching truck and a babble of human voices which lightened her anxiety. Ward had brought the Caribs to safety!

A dozen or more children poured out of the truck as it came to a halt on the gravelled drive before the main door, but Ward was not with them. One of the overseers on the estate saluted her.

'The boss, he go in search of Miss Salty,' he informed her. 'He go down to the harbour to look along the shore.'

Luella had unpacked the mini-moke.

'Put the parrots where they won't make too much noise,' Andrina advised. 'I'm going back to search along the ridge. If Mr Prentice comes home, Luella, tell him I think I know where Miss Salty may have gone. She had a "secret place" on the mountain, a cave of some sort, I think.'

'Why would she go there when that devil mountain spewed fire?' Luella demanded. 'She'd be sure afraid, Miss Drina, an' no mistake!'

'I've thought of that,' Andrina confessed, 'but I have to search. Something must have happened to her when the donkey came back alone.'

Reversing the mini-moke, she drove back through the spice grove where the air seemed hotter than ever. Every now and then there was an ominous rumble in the distance, as if of thunder, but now she knew that it came from far beneath the earth's crust. The mountain was shouting a warning.

She could not imagine why Salty should have gone there, but the impression persisted in her mind that the child had been riding towards Castaways. Beyond the shade of the spice grove the heat was intensified and the mini-moke seemed more reluctant to take the incline than before. A pall of smoke still hung over the nearer peak, billowing in a mushroom shape above the volcanic cone, while further off a glow of fire rimmed the northern crater's edge. Poor Salty, Andrina thought, she must be terrified.

Pressing her foot down on the accelerator with renewed determination, she approached the ridge. High up here above the plantations and the trees, she could see most of the island and it looked very much the same. She could see Tamarind Cove and the still water of the lagoon lying in the shelter behind the reef, and the thick growth of coconut palms which hid Castaways. She could also see the white coral sands of the north beach and, across the ridge, the black stretch of L'Anse Deux Feux lying open to the Atlantic swell. Between them the high Bluff with the two conical peaks which formed the mountain stood out against the horizon like black paper-cuts in the almost blinding light of the sun. But for the overpowering heat and the menacing plume of smoke nothing seemed changed, yet change was everywhere. The island was about to die.

Ward wasn't the kind of person to panic, but he had decided to evacuate the villages along the ridge which might lie in the path of the molten lava stream and the vulnerable coast area where the fishermen lived. He had accepted the fact that his half-completed harbour would go, smashed to pieces by the colossal tidal wave which followed an eruption, and he had made provision for that, too. Everything and everyone was more or less accounted for— except Salty.

Andrina looked about her, standing on the spot where she had met the child when she had gone with Gerry to look at the spring, remembering how Salty had pointed vaguely in the direction of the rocky mountainside which surrounded the nearer peak.

'It's in there,' she had said. 'A sort of cave . . .' But where, exactly? It was unthinkable to imagine that Salty was still hiding in a cave which could be in the path of the lethal stream of lava, but at least she must find out.

Leaving the mini-moke at the side of the narrow road, she took a path which wound upwards, calling Salty's name at intervals when she stopped to draw breath. The strong smell of sulphur coming from the volcano stung her nostrils and her hair lay straight and dank against her brow, but she struggled on.

'Salty!' she managed again. 'Salty, are you there?'

Imagining a faint cry which sounded barely human, she paused for a moment, aware of the heat beneath her feet now and the close proximity of the mountain which seemed to have taken on a demonic presence in the last half-hour. This is fear, she thought; this is what makes the Caribs talk of devils!

'Salty! Salty!'

The distant cry came again, nearer now. It came from the jutting rocks ahead of her, and she ran the last few feet towards the entrance to the cave. It was a shallow aperture, no more than a fissure in the rock, and she saw Salty lying there even before the child was aware of her.

'Oh, Salty——!' she cried in relief, gathering the little girl into her arms as she sank to her knees on the hard ground.

Salty clung to her in silence, struggling with the tears she would not shed.

'I was coming to look for you,' she said, at last, in a shaken voice. 'I was coming to Castaways.'

'What happened to the donkey?' Andrina found herself asking for want of something better to say.

'He ran away.' There was a sob in Salty's voice now. 'When I slipped he ran away.' One hand went down to her ankle. 'It hurt, but I didn't cry.'

'Let me look at it.' Andrina had noticed the swollen foot. 'What happened?'

'I fell. We heard the thunder and I fell off Pedro's back. He didn't wait for me because he was frightened,' she added, trying to be brave.

It was impossible not to think about the agony of fear Salty herself must have suffered when she found herself alone on the mountain with the fire from the crater glowing against the sky almost above her head, but the practical thing was to examine the injured foot and decide what to do. The volcano had quietened, but there was still the malevolent glow over the nearer crater to remind them of the mountain's wrath.

'I think you've sprained your ankle,' Andrina said, helping the child to her feet. 'Try to walk a little way.'

Salty did her best, but it was evident that she was in pain.

'We'll make it to the Moke,' said Andrina. 'Climb on my back.'

'You'll fall,' Salty predicted, her wide blue eyes fixed on the mountain.

'No, I'm very strong. Put your arms round my neck and I'll give you a piggyback.'

Salty giggled.

'That's a funny thing to say! You're not a pig.'

'It's just something we say in England,' Andrina explained. 'It's a good way to carry someone who's been hurt.'

Salty's arms tightened about her neck.

'I love you very much,' she said. 'I was coming to tell you.'

Strictly speaking, she was no great weight and it was no distance to the mini-moke, but Andrina arrived there out of breath.

'Here we are!' she said, lowering her burden to the ground. 'Hold on till I can help you in.'

The mini-moke was as stubborn as Pedro. It refused to start. As if it had expended all its energy in the effort to climb the dirt track, it coughed and sputtered as she tried the starter but refused to go. In the end Andrina said carefully:

'Salty, we'll have to walk. I'll help you all I can.'

Salty glanced at the mountain, nodding her agreement. The mini-moke would have to be left behind because they were wasting precious time, but with any luck they would meet someone on the way over the ridge, either Ward come to look for them or one of the overseers with a truckful of Caribs from an outlying settlement. It didn't matter which.

In her heart Andrina knew that she wanted it to be Ward. She needed his strength and encouragement more than anything else and she also needed his approval, but if she could get Salty back to Nettleton's that would lighten his burden of responsibility, if nothing else.

The steep mountain road was downhill most of the way, which was a considerable help, but by the time she had reached the tree line she was exhausted. Salty wasn't a heavy child, but the heat was oppressive and very soon beads of perspiration were standing on her forehead and along the line of her upper lip. Twice she wiped them away with the back of her hand, trying to keep up a conversation which would steer Salty's thoughts away from the volcano, but it became more and more difficult to disregard the mountain as it growled and spat its wrath on to the rocks beneath the crater rim.

The spice grove seemed to recede farther and farther away as she struggled on with Salty's hot little hands grasping her neck in an unconscious stranglehold, and once she allowed the child to slip to the ground so that she could breathe freely, supporting her with an arm round her shoulders.

'We'll sit down for a while once we get to the trees,' she promised. 'We're almost there.'

The spice grove was sanctuary even if it was only from the too fierce heat of the sun.

'Salty, we can do it!' she cried. 'We have only a short way to go now.'

The overpowering scent of nutmeg hung heavily on the air, mingling with the smell of cinnamon to make her senses reel, but they obliterated the sulphurous breath of the volcano which had threatened to choke her on the mountainside. A thin powdering of ash drifted down to settle like a grey pall on the trees, and she realised for the first time that her hair and clothes were covered in it. When Salty brushed her hand across her brow it left a dark streak of ash and sweat on her hairline and she probably looked much the same.

'It's baths all round when we get to Nettleton's,' she tried to say cheerfully, although they had still a long way to go before they reached the shelter of the estate house.

Ten minutes later they were out of the grove and trudging through the banana plantation where the ragged foliage gave them a certain amount of shelter from the sun. The mountain growled again, sending a plume of smoke so high into the air that they could see it plainly against the sky.

'It's going to blow,' Salty said between her teeth, using Garson's expression for an eruption.

'Not yet,' Andrina said defiantly. 'We'll make it!'

She staggered out of the plantation at last, hardly conscious of the direction she took, yet moving instinctively towards Nettleton's. Salty's arms tightened about her neck. A man was coming towards them from the direction of the house and Andrina looked up with Ward's name on her lips, but it wasn't Ward.

'Daddy!' Salty cried, loosening her grip. 'Oh, Daddy, you've come back!'

The man was so like Ward to look at that Andrina could only stare at him in silence for a moment until a wave of overwhelming relief swept everything else from her mind.

'You're Richard,' she said as he came forward to take his daughter into his arms. 'How did you get here?'

'I heard you were in trouble and naturally I made for Grenada.' He pressed Salty's dust-covered head against his shoulder. 'One thing about a volcano, it signals its intentions for everybody to see. The pall of smoke was visible long before we reached Grenada and I was able to pick up a launch in St George's. But first things first,' he added, his voice not quite steady as he looked down at his daughter for the first time in many months. 'What have you been doing to yourself in my absence, my girl? And perhaps you could introduce me to your friend.'

Overcome by surprise and delight, Salty remained speechless, her face buried in the soft folds of his shirt as if it had always been there.

'I'm Andrina Collington and I really belong at Castaways, but when the mountain threatened to blow Ward decided we should come over here,' Andrina explained.

'I haven't seen him,' Richard Prentice said, 'but I expect he'll need our help. What happened to your foot?' he asked Salty.

'Pedro threw me and ran away. He's a donkey,' his daughter explained. 'Fair stubborn,' she added for his further enlightenment.

'I see.' He carried her easily. 'I think we'd better make it to the house.'

Pandemonium reigned at Nettleton's. There were far too many people to accommodate under one roof and they spilled into the garden, across the terracing and half-way down the hillside, but they believed themselves to be safe and that was the main thing. Luella and Berthe, with a dozen willing helpers, were dispensing cooling drinks and honey cakes to the children, while all the men seemed to have disappeared.

'They must have gone to help Ward,' Richard Prentice decided when he had strapped up Salty's ankle. 'Will you put her to bed?'

Andrina nodded, wondering about Ward.

'You'll come back, Richard?' she asked. 'You'll tell me what's happened?'

'Sure!' He gave her a long, searching look. 'No harm can have come to him.'

'He may still be searching for Salty,' she said. 'Find him and tell him she's safe.'

'I'll do that.' He kissed his daughter on the brow. 'Be good, infant!' he said gently.

He's come to stay, Andrina thought, for as long as Ward needs him.

When Salty was finally asleep there seemed to be nothing to do but wait. Darkness fell and with it a respite in the noise from the mountain, an almost ominous hush. Kerosene flares were lit as if in defiance of the volcano's fury, although the Caribs were still afraid. They gathered into groups, sitting cross-legged on the rough grass or crouched along the terrace wall, and, presently they began to chant. It was a strange, dirge-like sound, seeming to come from the very depth of the earth, oddly disturbing in its intensity.

Luella came to bring Andrina a drink.

'Soon the wave will come,' she said philosophically. 'Then it be all over.'

'Luella!' Andrina gripped her by the arm. 'Where do you think the men have gone?'

'Mr Prentice an' de brother? I think they go to de harbour.'

'But the wave? You said just now that it would come. How can you be sure?'

'Because it always come. De volcano he blow an' de wave come. It sweep everythin' away down there.' She pointed in the general direction of the harbour. 'Maybe Mr Prentice come quick up here where it is safe.'

Ward and Richard would be down there together; Andrina felt sure of that. They were brothers and Flambeau mattered to them. That was part of the reason why Richard had come back.

As dawn broke a dull explosion shook the island. It seemed to come from the ground beneath their feet, shattering the comparative peace of Nettleton's where some of the settlers were asleep. Andrina, who had not gone to bed, rushed on to the terrace, but apart from the startled birds there was nothing to be seen or heard. Then, very faintly, in the mysterious half-light, she saw an enormous plume of smoke rising above the trees. It spiralled for several minutes before it seemed to break away from its stalk to float gently above the ocean, a gigantic cloud with no fire in it, the breath of a volcano that was already spent.

She rushed to Salty's bedroom, but the child was fast asleep, impervious to any sound, her fair hair still dulled by the ash which had dropped so stealthily on them while they struggled back to Nettleton's.

As the light strengthened the Caribs began to stir.

'They want to go back to their homes,' Berthe said. 'I make them big breakfast, then they go!'

The emergency was over, but where was Ward? Down on the shore with his brother fighting off the tidal wave which they had neither seen nor heard? Or had he gone once again to the mountain to persuade the last of the Caribs to come to Nettleton's and safety?

Andrina could no longer remain in the house, a sense of urgency goading her to make her way to the nearest plantation. If either Ward or Richard had been injured she might be able to help, but once she had reached the spice grove it was too dark among the trees to see clearly and she was forced to turn back.

Pinpoints of light shed by the lamps Berthe had lit

guided her towards the terrace and soon she could hear the
babble of voices. Shadowy figures hovered on the terrace
steps and one of them was Ward. Ward or Richard. They
were devastatingly alike.

'Ward!' she exclaimed, holding out her hand. 'I tried to
find you——'

She saw him plainly then and there could be no mistaking the look in his eyes. Whatever the future held for him
now that his brother had returned she could only think of
him as the master of Nettleton's. Apart from the fact that
his shirt was torn and a thin trickle of blood oozed from a
gash on his forehead, he was the same as he had always
been, assured and purposeful, the man who would tackle
any situation and expect to win. Then she saw him more
clearly, the fatigue which bowed his strong shoulders and
the weariness in his eyes. He had worked all day and
throughout the night to save an island which might no
longer be his.

'Let me look after you,' she said, taking a step towards
him.

'I asked you to do that once before.' His voice was suddenly harsh.

'You asked me to look after Salty,' she corrected him.
'There's a difference.'

'You mean you would marry me without giving it a
second thought?' There was a gleam in his eyes which she
recognised. 'On the strength of my need for someone to
look after me?'

'No.' She drew in a deep breath. 'I don't like ghosts.'

He looked at her intently.

'Ghosts?'

'Salty's mother. You were in love with her.'

He didn't deny it, but she saw his mouth harden.

'Nola is dead,' he said. 'She has no place in my life now.'

'You couldn't be sure.'

'I *am* sure.' His hands gripped her arms, turning her to
face him. 'Why did you come here?' he demanded. 'Had
you a problem to work out?'

'Yes.'

'And it's still unresolved?'

'I don't know.'

'You must have been very deeply in love,' he said. 'You're that sort of person. Are you going back to him?'

She shook her head.

'It wasn't that sort of affair,' she declared. 'He just decided to marry someone else—after three years.' She looked at him in the rapidly strengthening light. 'So you see, I'm not ready to try again where there's any doubt.'

His grip on her arms tightened.

'Do you want me to promise undying affection?' he demanded. 'Do you want me to say I've never loved anyone in my life before?' He held her closely so that she could feel the strong beating of his heart under the torn shirt. 'Perhaps I could even do that,' he added. 'What I felt for Nola was affection and a wild regret when she finally married my brother, but when I came to my senses and realised what sort of person she was all that changed to guilt because I had brought her to Flambeau in the first place.' His lips were almost on her mouth, but he still held her wavering gaze. 'You wanted the truth,' he said. 'I stayed here because I believed I owed Salty a home when Richard couldn't face things after Nola's death. It's different now. He wants to live on Barbados, to make a home for her so that she can go to school like any ordinary kid.'

'Ward——'

She pressed the palms of her hands against his taut brown body, but he took them both in one of his, sweeping her words aside.

'I love you,' he said purposefully. 'When are you going to realise it and give in? I'm not asking you to marry me right away—you can take your time to consider it, if you must—but there doesn't seem to be any good reason why we shouldn't make the decision now. We can sail off on *Sea Hawk* and be home to see your aunt safely back at Castaways in a month's time.'

His lips came down firmly on hers in a kiss which drained

all her doubts away and the garden was suddenly bright
with the joy of a new day.

'What is it to be?' he asked. 'Now, or in some distant
future when I've fully proved my love?'

Her hand went up to caress his dark cheek.

'Now, Ward,' she said. 'Now and for ever.'

He drew her to the terrace edge to where they could look
down across the ravine to the distant harbour which he had
built.

'Most of it has gone,' he said, 'but I can build it up again.
The tidal wave was smaller than we thought. If you look
over there you can see the result of all this turmoil.'

At the edge of L'Anse Deux Feux Andrina could see a
vague shadow resting on the surface of the ocean, a long,
low outline which hadn't been there before.

'Another island,' said Ward, drawing her close again. 'It
sometimes happens when a volcano erupts under the sea. It
can't be any use to Flambeau for a long time, but eventually we'll be able to grow crops there and maybe build a
causeway to make a bigger harbour.'

They were looking out to the east, facing the sun at
the beginning of a new day, and suddenly the sky was
brilliant with the pink aftermath of dawn. It seemed to
Andrina that they were looking straight into the future.

They turned away at last, Ward's arm strong about her
shoulders, and on the terrace at their feet they saw a small
seedling tree. Ward stooped to pick it up.

'I wonder where that was blown from,' he said, turning
it over in his hand to inspect the roots. 'It's sturdy enough.
We'll plant it where we can see it from the house and watch
it grow.'

Like our love, Andrina thought, resting her head on his
shoulder. All these years until it's a great, strong tree!

Harlequin understands...

the way you feel about love

Harlequin novels are stories of people in love—people like you— and all are beautiful romances, set in exotic faraway places.

Harlequin Presents...

Romance novels that speak
the language of love known to
women the world over.

Harlequin Presents...

A distinctive series of dramatic
love stories created
especially for you
by world-acclaimed
authors.

Harlequin Romances

The books that let you escape
into the wonderful world of romance!
Trips to exotic places...interesting
plots...meeting memorable people...
the excitement of love.... These are
integral parts of Harlequin Romances—
the heartwarming novels read by
women everywhere.

Many early issues are now available.
Choose from this great selection!

Choose from this list of Harlequin Romance editions.*

*Some of these book were originally published under different titles.

Relive a great love story...
with Harlequin Romances
Complete and mail this coupon today!

Harlequin Reader Service

In U.S.A.
MPO Box 707
Niagara Falls, N.Y. 14302

In Canada
649 Ontario St.
Stratford, Ontario, N5A 6W2

Please send me the following Harlequin Romance novels. I am enclosing my check or money order for $1.25 for each novel ordered, plus 59¢ to cover postage and handling.

☐ 422	☐ 509	☐ 636	☐ 729	☐ 810	☐ 902
☐ 434	☐ 517	☐ 673	☐ 737	☐ 815	☐ 903
☐ 459	☐ 535	☐ 663	☐ 746	☐ 838	☐ 909
☐ 481	☐ 559	☐ 684	☐ 748	☐ 872	☐ 920
☐ 492	☐ 583	☐ 713	☐ 798	☐ 878	☐ 927
☐ 508	☐ 634	☐ 714	☐ 799	☐ 888	☐ 941

Number of novels checked @ $1.25 each = $_____

N.Y. and Ariz. residents add appropriate sales tax. $_____

Postage and handling $_____.59

TOTAL $_____

I enclose _____
(Please send check or money order. We cannot be responsible for cash sent through the mail.)

Prices subject to change without notice.

NAME _____
(Please Print)

ADDRESS _____

CITY _____

STATE/PROV. _____

ZIP/POSTAL CODE _____

Offer expires January 31, 1982.   105563371